Abduction
In Haifa

E. Allen Stewart III

Order this book online at www.trafford.com
or email orders@trafford.com

Most Trafford titles are also available at major online book retailers.

Front cover and sketches by Margaret O'Leary.

Images by Spencer Pullen of Premier Graphics, Inc.

Printed in the United States of America.

ISBN: 978-1-4669-7051-9 (sc)
ISBN: 978-1-4669-7053-3 (hc)
ISBN: 978-1-4669-7052-6 (e)

Library of Congress Control Number: 2012922395

Trafford rev. 03/01/2013

Trafford PUBLISHING® www.trafford.com

North America & international
toll-free: 1 888 232 4444 (USA & Canada)
phone: 250 383 6864 ♦ fax: 812 355 4082

In memory of

Alex Padva
A peace loving citizen of Israel and a friend never to be forgotten

and

Icy and Milton Miller
The parents of my wife June who exemplified the grace and
friendliness of the people of the great State of Alabama.
The memory of their lives will be cherished always

Acknowledgements

It has always seemed appropriate that any expression of gratitude for contributions related to anything I might create, or imagine, or strive to understand not be limited to those with whom I have enjoyed direct contact. So many great artists, scientists, leaders and philosophers have through their acts of genius provided me the freedom and understanding to pursue my creative urges, and for this I will always be grateful. And even though I have never met any of these people, they have been so important in my personal development. Among these are the great peacemakers Lao-Tsu, Jesus and Muhammad, and during recent times Teddy Roosevelt, Gandhi, the Dalai Lama, Martin Luther King Jr., Jimmy Carter, Anwar Sadat, Yitzhak Rabin and Nelson Mandela; the scientists and philosophers such as Descartes, Darwin, Huxley, Wallace, Einstein, the Leakey Family, Christopher Hitchens, Alan Watts, Daniel Quinn, Jane Goodall, Richard Dawkins, H.T. Odum, Stephen Jay Gould, Jared Diamond, and E.O. Wilson; the strong political leaders of the United States, Washington, Franklin, Jefferson, Adams, Madison, Lincoln, FDR, Truman, Eisenhower, JFK, Colin Powell, the Clintons, and Barack Obama; and the great composers and literary talents such as Shakespeare, Beethoven, Mozart, Brahms, Tchaikovsky, T.S. Elliot, Robert Frost, Tolstoy, Shostakovich, Bernstein, Gershwin, Copeland, John Lennon, Paul Simon, Jimmy Buffet and Carl Hiaasen.

Personally I owe so much to the small collection of people who have been able to tolerate my lack of social skills and my often abrasive and aloof personality in an effort to remain my friend. Gary Bartlett, Herb Zebuth, Whit Palmer, Mark Zivojnovich, John Sikes, Mahmoud Najda, and Keith McCully have had to endure my abuses the longest, for I have known them for decades, and remain amazed at their ability to tolerate and forgive. Each has taught me important lessons in life, and for this I will always be grateful.

More recent friends are Robinson Bazurto, Buddy, MacKay, Matt and Yoshi Van Ert, Gordon Pickett, Marta Eagle and Ric Welle, Chuck and Linda Sue Gertner, David and Charlie Gertner, Tina Narr, Linde and Trish O'Connell, Valerie Alker and Larry (Coop) Cooper, John and Linda Dobrian, Debbie and Rick Highsmith, Sara Lee and Howard Banaszak, all of the folks associated with Camp Boggy Creek in Lake County, Florida, where my wife June serves as CEO, and Betty and Hal Warlick and Bonnie Wacker, our Spartanburg connections. I have enjoyed my relationship with each of them, and hopefully, depending upon their level of tolerance, these relationships will continue to grow.

I am thankful for my two sons—Thomas Wayne Stewart and A.J. Stewart—and my two grandsons, Tristan and T.J. Stewart, all of whom bring joy into my life. My sister Margaret who reminds me so much of my mother Mickey, is both talented and joyfully optimistic, and has contributed so much to my life. I am thankful also for her husband Steve O'Leary and their daughter Erin for loving Margaret as they do. I am blessed as well with an extended Alabama Family, thanks to my wife June, a native of Birmingham. One could not find more loving and giving people. Finally, I am totally inspired by the support and love my wife June has given me over the years. She is a remarkable spirit who brings a level of understanding of the human condition that has helped me immensely. I would be a lonely misfit without her.

CHAPTER 1

Haifa, she had been in Haifa! was the woman's first thought as she regained consciousness. As her senses returned, she noticed that a light was shining in her eyes and that there was an awful smell of human body odor and stale garlic. The source of the smell became clear when she realized two large men, who appeared very Middle Eastern, both in countenance and clothing, were carrying her by her arms, with her legs dragging behind them. The light she presumed was from the powerful light held by one of the men. She then noticed they were in some type of cavern-like room. In terror, she recognized she was being kidnapped.

She screamed and attempted to pull away. Both efforts had little influence on the men, who seemed determined to hasten her delivery to somewhere or to someone.

"Let me go! Where are you taking me?" And then she started crying, hysterically crying, and then she began screaming. Her emotional collapse solicited no change in the posture or intent of purpose within the men. Before falling again into unconsciousness, she thought about Haifa. It was safe, she was told. Apparently not so! Someone must have been convinced that this middle-aged, middle-class woman from Indiana was worth kidnapping—that she would bring a decent ransom or could be used to coerce the release of some terrorist from an Israeli prison.

Time has no meaning to the unconscious, so Martha had no way of knowing how long she had been lying on the ground. She knew she had fainted not because of injury but because of sheer terror. Now aware again, she felt the terror enveloping her mind. She screamed because the fear forced her to scream. She screamed loudly and without restraint, hoping perhaps the sound would reach the ears of someone willing to help her or would solicit some sympathy from those who held her. The screams came from a part of her that found its origins and directives from an ancient past, from the distant beginnings of her genetic history, forcing her to make all efforts to survive.

When it became obvious the screaming was futile, she thought of escape. But the terror had seized her muscles; she could hardly move. She simply collapsed and shook. She wished she could escape the crippling control of her fear. She wished she could again gain some respite through unconsciousness. And then she prayed. It did not dissolve the fear.

"You urinated on yourself, Mrs. Browning. It is not an uncommon thing when people think they are about to die. Do you think you are going to die, Mrs. Browning?"

The voice, it was accented, but the English was very clear and concise. The message was ominous, but hearing words in English offered a wisp of comfort. Still terrified, she felt at least no more escalation in her fear. Panic was not going to work; perhaps she needed to try to mitigate the fear and try rational thought. It was not easy to do, however. She felt herself trying to speak.

She did not answer the question, however, but understandably started with a series of questions of her own. "Who are you? What do you want from me?" she said in a tone she knew further revealed her fear, not that she had been trying to keep it a secret that she was scared, scared to an extent she never imagined was possible. She then again fell into unconsciousness.

During this second period of unconsciousness, Martha had a dream—or more correctly, a recollection. She was an eighteen-year-old, just starting as a freshman at the University of Florida. It was 1976. The recollection was not about any specific event that occurred during this period of her life. Rather, it was more of a review of feelings she had during that time. The dominant feelings were insecurity and a sense of inferiority—certainly feelings not unusual for a naive young girl reared in a small Southern city. But for some reason, as these feelings impinged their influence upon her thoughts, she felt, for the first time, shame and guilt. She felt shame and guilt because she had been timid and uncertain, because she had not allowed her ambitions to emerge from their hiding place in her mind, because she did not protest as her libido was flogged into submission by her parents and her teachers, because at such an early age, a socially sculpted identity had been forced upon her—and she had accepted it and embraced it and paid for it with all the innate sense of creativity and imagination she possessed. Her existence was rigidly solidified by those formative years, and her life became predictable, unexciting, but safe. It was the easy way out, and now she was, for the first time in her life, contemplating this submission, and feeling ashamed and guilty for denying herself the joy of developing her own identity and for not purging herself of the stifling encumbrances that she had accepted so readily.

CHAPTER 2

Martha had been fraught with mixed feelings about visiting the Holy Lands. Her church, which organized the trip, was encouraging those who could afford it to visit Israel so they could track the life of Jesus through Bethlehem and Nazareth and the Sea of Galilee and, of course, Jerusalem. The preacher had delivered a most moving sermon about how a trip to the Holy Land prepares the soul for eternal life and brings one closer to God and to Jesus.

Martha wanted badly to go to Israel. She wanted to bring Jesus even closer into her life, and her preacher did not have to do much persuading to convince her that this trip would certainly make this happen. But another side of her was filled with anxiety. The violence in Israel seemed to persist, and with Netanyahu re-elected as prime minister, tensions had increased. The Palestinians—in fact, much of the Arab world—seemed to hate this man. In Indiana, she did not think much about this. But to actually plan to go to this place where people were killed by bombs and gun battles in the street was frightening.

And now she knew why, for she had been kidnapped! Martha Browning, a harmless, somewhat shallow person from middle-America—kidnapped by Arab terrorists. It could not be real, but it was, for here she was, sitting on damp soil in some type of hideout with only enough light to reflect shadowy forms. And she was surrounded by filth! The smell of garlic and spices and urine and body odor and noxious gases—all of whose origins she did not even want to think about. She tried to stand, but it only forced her to vomit.

"Drink this water, Mrs. Browning."

How did they know her name? Well, that's easy, they had her purse. They knew as much about her by now as the FBI. She began crying again, then commenced heavy sobbing with short, terror-filled screams. She wanted to die. Get it over with.

"Yes, I think I am going to die. Do it quickly, please, with no pain!" she finally screamed.

"Whether you live or die is your choice, Mrs. Browning."

"If I have to stay here with these smells and with you disgusting people, then I would rather die!" she said with contempt as she pulled herself to her feet. She charged the man facing her and struck him in the face. He did not flinch. As she slipped, she grabbed his clothing. He did not move as she pulled herself to her feet. The smell of this man, of this place, was overwhelming.

"Do you really mean that, do you really want to die?"

She thought about the prospect of actually dying. She had never faced this possibility before, so she was confused. But more than confused, she was scared; she was petrified by fear.

"I do not want to die," she confessed quietly, almost shamefully.

Why am I so frightened of dying? she asked herself. *Should I not believe that Jesus will be there when I die to take me to everlasting life? This is what I have professed over and over again. Why am I so frightened if I am convinced that eternal life is my fate? Do I have doubts? Perhaps I do. Regardless, whatever the reason, be it doubts or just innate fear, I do not want to die—not now.*

"I do not want to die!" she screamed.

"Why not?" was the man's curious inquisition.

"What do you mean, why not? Nobody wants to die," she responded quickly.

"Are you sure about that?" was the reply.

The man chuckled and then turned to leave. He stopped before walking away and returned to Martha and gave her a bowl of water.

"You need to drink if you really do not want to die," he said.

She took the bowl. She shuddered to think what the water looked like and how dirty it might be. She drank it anyway, for she was incredibly thirsty. It was bitter with a bit of sweetness. She knew almost immediately it was poisoned or, at least, drugged. And she was not surprised when she soon became dizzy, disoriented. *Am I going to die?* The drug had overwhelmed her fear. She did not care. All she wanted to do was sleep, and she did.

The sleep was not a normal sleep, however. Apparently, the drug was somewhat hallucinogenic. Very real dreams, recollections, sped into her mind with such velocity that she could hardly recognize their content. They appeared to be about her life. She saw her first clumsy attempt at sex; her inability to communicate and her feelings of inadequacy; her first marriage and her first child and the abuse; her divorce and her expression of sexual freedom afterward; her vulnerability to people, mostly men, and the price she paid for submitting to their influences; her second marriage and the growing distance between her and her first child, a bright but frail and confused boy; the pains of trying to orchestrate life encumbered by the mutual hatred between her son and her second husband; the second divorce; the death of her parents; her drinking; her desperation; her grasping on to the church as a last hope for happiness and understanding; the long struggle to become sober and to gain some self-respect; her third marriage; and finally, complacency, blessed complacency, which eased her mind. She let her burdens, all the demons, which played in her mind, go to Jesus, and it gave her peace of mind, for she finally had an explanation. *I may be a loser, but Jesus does not care. He loves me anyway, and as long as I give myself to him, I will be loved, I will be saved. I am assured a place in heaven, and I can have peace while I am on earth.* It was all the assurance she needed. Her demons were gone, as was her spirit. With her third husband, she could now relax and finish out her life.

So why did she feel she had to come to Israel? She had fallen into the same trap—convinced to do something she knew deep inside was not what she should do. But her preacher, whom she adored, had been so convincing. Only after she got to Israel did she find out he received 10 percent of the fee from the company that organized and conducted the tour. It made her angry and disappointed.

But Israel soon made her forget her anger. There was an authenticity about Israel that permeated every aspect of the indigenous cultures—Jewish, Muslim, Christian, Hebrew, Arabs, and Druze. And the people—none of them fit the common stereotypes. The Jews were not abrupt and cheap; the Arabs were not callous and slovenly. In fact, there seemed a common decency among most of the people that she did not really see that often in Indiana. It was puzzling to her. How could people be so aware, so friendly, and so giving and yet be involved in such violence and hatred? She began to recognize the issues such as those related to the Middle East are much more complex and multifaceted than what is presented in the American press. And for the first time in her life, she became curious and concerned about issues outside of her immediate sphere of existence. She saw that she was indeed connected to these problems, that the fate of these people was intertwined with her fate. It not only made her feel better about herself but also, in a way she did not quite understand, more responsible for the future.

CHAPTER 3

hil, what must Phil be thinking right now—what actions is he taking to save her? Martha thought. Phil, her third husband of nearly ten years, was not in favor of her coming to Israel. "Jews and Arabs—good God, woman, what are you thinking! You know they all hate us Christians. The Jews killed Jesus, and the Muslims took the Holy Land away from the rightful owners—Christians," Phil had warned. (Phil made no distinction between Arabs and Muslims, like many Americans.) Coming to Israel had not received Phil's blessing. But then she did not think it would. He was, in essence, a bigot, convinced of the evil and dishonesty of everyone except middle-class white Christian Americans. But Martha went anyway, and now, it looked as though Phil's concerns were quite valid.

Martha was recovering from the drug that had been given to her. She was lying on the ground on a thick blanket. Someone had changed her clothes, which now consisted of only a rough wool dress and a baggy cotton blouse. She had no undergarments on at all. Opening her eyes, she noticed the same man talking to a group of people—both men and women—at the far side of the cave. She found it interesting that the women covered their hair but were not veiled—not what you would expect from a Muslim extremist.

"What did you give me, and who changed my clothes?" she asked in a faint but indignant voice.

The same man, who was the apparent leader of the group, lifted his head to respond. "Mrs. Browning, the first rule is that only we ask questions. Who we are is not information we wish to share with you. Regarding your clothes, I will tell you that these women were the only ones involved. Trust me, you did not want to keep your old clothes."

His gaze sent a shiver down her spine. This man, she was convinced, was pure evil. His eyes penetrated all the way to her soul. *Whatever a soul is*, she thought.

"You are Hezbollah, aren't you?" she asked. She knew that Haifa was close to Lebanon—they had to be Hezbollah. Although she did not recall many recent news stories about Hezbollah kidnapping westerners, she was sure it had happened. But why would Hezbollah do this? The Israeli army had long left Lebanon, and the 2006 conflict was resolved years ago.

The man laughed. "What do you know about Hezbollah?"

"They are Lebanese Shiite Muslim terrorists!" she shouted. "Just as you are."

"Oh, so I am Muslim? Why do you think that?" he said.

"Who else would be involved in such a kidnapping?" she snapped back.

"CIA maybe or the Israeli Mossad. Maybe Jewish radicals. Maybe Christian radicals," he said.

"I never heard of Christian radicals!" she shouted. "That is absurd."

"Tell that to the Palestinian refugees or the native peoples of the New World or the African slaves or to the Muslims attacked during the crusades or to the Vietnamese Buddhists or to those killed by bombs in England by Irish rebels," he replied.

"That was different," she replied, although she knew it was not really any different.

"Besides, that was a long time ago—Christians are different today."

"Different? How?" he asked.

"Christians today have a deep belief in Jesus and in the Holy Trinity. Jesus did not teach hate," she said.

"Neither did Muhammad the Prophet—peace be upon him" he answered. "But there is still plenty of hate on all sides. Why is that?"

Martha began crying again, not because of the conversation, but because she again recognized the reality of her situation. This man was intimidating with his banter and his directness. "I don't know!" she screamed. "I just don't know—I am just a simple woman from Indiana. Please, let me go, let me go back to my family." She had fallen again into hysteria.

"You know I cannot do that," the man said. But Martha did not hear him. She had lost consciousness again.

CHAPTER 4

With the loss of consciousness came the dreams again, although they were different this time. She was a young child, and she was playing in a spring—one of those cool clear springs that dotted the central Florida landscape in the sixties. The bottom was covered with eel grass that swayed in the current and, in combination with the light, offered a hypnotic but soothing rhythm. It was summertime, and the sounds of cicadas enveloped everything in a constant shrill. In spite of the heat, the springwater would set off shivers and goose bumps after about fifteen minutes, forcing one to move out into the sunshine on the bank, like a basking cooter. Dragonflies scurried around the marsh plants, hunting and occasionally dropping eggs into the water. In the shade, the brilliantly colored damselflies rested on stems just above the water, and whirlygigs and striders maintained constant motion on the surface. Gold Speckled Top Minnows darted around the maiden cane, searching constantly for mosquito larvae and small crustaceans while protecting their little piece of submerged territory from other intruding top minnows. A small ribbon snake ventured

11

into the open water, finding a convenient willow branch on the other side. There it seemed content to remain, perhaps resting after swallowing a spring peeper or a tree frog. This was a typical Florida day in Martha's childhood. It was so comforting, so interesting.

But soon the spring started to fade until it totally disappeared. Martha found herself in an open field covered in dog fennel, Spanish needles, and sandspurs. The sun beat down, spilling unbearable heat upon her exposed body. She looked in all directions but could see nothing—nothing except a skinny, sickly dog that limped toward her. It gazed at her with pathetic eyes, looking as if it were about to give up its last spark of life. The dog had large sores on its body that gave off a smell of decomposing flesh. The dog was disgusting, and while she felt somewhat sympathetic, she could only shrink from its ugliness. She turned and ran, looking back only once to see the dog glaring back at her in confusion.

Martha awoke with a start—she had forgotten about that dog long ago—at least, she thought she had. For some reason, her mind chose now to remind her of that encounter. It had to be the drugs. Was the dog symbolic of her selfishness? Certainly she had felt some guilt for leaving the dog to a certain death—but why this recollection now?

It was nighttime, and the only light she saw was a small lingering fire. She could hear sleeping bodies all around. She thought of escape, but escape to where? She had no idea how to get out of this cave. Perhaps she could see some light from outside. She stood up and walked quietly toward what she had remembered as the entrance to the room. She strained to look out the passageway but could see nothing but darkness. She again started weeping, although quietly this time, as someone who recognized that there would be no escape from fear. Even with sleep, the dreams brought anxiety. Martha sat down, pulled her knees around her, and just sat, continuing to cry. Maybe tomorrow would bring new opportunities for escape. Perhaps Phil would come tomorrow and rescue her. Before long, into spite of her anxieties, Martha fell into a deep sleep.

CHAPTER 5

Martha was surprised at how well she slept. In fact, she would have likely slept for another hour or so had she not been awoken by a gentle tapping on her shoulder. Upon opening her eyes, she focused upon a young lady dressed in simple clothes, smiling at her.

"Must go," the lady said. "Work today."

It was obvious to Martha that this person did not understand English, for the words fell clumsily out of her mouth, indicating they were simply memorized. Martha, still transitioning to full consciousness, studied the lady's face. Even with her hair covered and without the help of makeup, her beauty was obvious. Her eyes were almost black but very clear. They were surrounded by olive skin free of wrinkles and accentuated by a flawless mouth and straight white teeth. Martha guessed she could not be more than twenty-five years old.

"Fatima," she said smiling, pointing to herself. "We go work!"

"Martha," she mimicked, pointing to herself. "Work where?"

It was clear that Fatima did not understand the question. Rather, she took Martha's hand and pulled her up. She led her to a hidden, isolated room with a small trench dug the length of the room, which Martha immediately recognized as the communal women's toilet. One portion of the trench held the past few days' deposits, which had been covered with lime. This succeeded in sequestering only a small fraction of the smell.

Martha gave Fatima a look of confusion and disgust. Fatima laughed and then straddled the trench herself, pulled up her dress, squatted slightly, and urinated. She then pointed to Martha, who responded with an audible sigh. Reluctantly, Martha proceeded to follow Fatima's lead. When she was finished, she pointed to her face and teeth, making a washing motion. Fatima nodded and then led her to a small connected room. Martha noticed a barrel of water supported by a crude pedestal. A shut-off valve placed on the bottom of the barrel facilitated access to the water. Several small bowls were stacked on a nearby table next to a few folded towels. A small bowl containing white powder had also been placed on the table. Martha assumed this was for cleaning her teeth. Understanding the implied procedure, Martha drew a bowl of water and, using one of the towels, washed her face and cleaned her teeth. Fatima handed her a cup of clean water. Martha took the cup and swished the water around her mouth and spat into the bowl. When she was finished, Fatima took the bowl and, walking into the toilet area, poured the contents into the trench. She washed the bowl with the remaining contents of the cup and then returned it to the small table.

Following Fatima from the latrine through the cave hallway, Martha's brain reminded her that she had been kidnapped. Fear again assaulted her being, and she stopped walking and began shaking and crying uncontrollably. When Fatima heard this, she stopped walking and returned to Martha's side, grabbing her just as she started to crumble. Instinctively, Martha collected herself and, sobbing, embraced Fatima.

"I'm so scared. What are they going to do with me?" she asked, realizing Fatima had no idea what she was saying.

Fatima spoke a few words in a soft voice, which Martha could not understand although she realized they were offered to comfort her. Fatima held Martha in this embrace for a full two minutes, repeating the words several times. Amazingly, her words did help calm Martha, allowing her to escape the threatening hysteria and to subdue her fear.

My abductors may be harsh, evil, and malodorous, thought Martha, *but Fatima is truly a good person—I am certain of this. Perhaps she was also kidnapped and has simply adjusted to life with these barbarians.*

Martha decided she would stay as close to Fatima as possible and would try to cultivate a real friendship with her.

Upon release of her embrace, Fatima took Martha's hand and guided her through a series of walkways and chambers until, finally, a small ray of sunlight presented itself. Fatima led Martha to a rather flimsy-looking ladder. Reluctantly, Martha followed her up the ladder, and as she climbed, she noted the intensity of the sunlight increasing. At the top of the ladder, Martha carefully stepped onto the floor and, upon lifting her head, gazed out the cavern entrance where she saw the emerging dawn spreading light over an expansive verdant valley.

CHAPTER 6

Martha had become a Christian out of convenience. Subconsciously, she knew that, but she never let that reality gain her full, overt recognition. When the thought would come to her, she would quickly dismiss it with a whispered denial or prayer. She suspected that many others in her church were also Christians for convenience. It was convenient because it stopped the questioning; it subdued the anxiety brought on by wondering about life's purpose and meaning or whether there even was a purpose or meaning. And of course, it softened the harshness of knowing your own mortality. The constant drumming of an active mind was silenced by that simple surrender to Jesus. A frontal lobotomy could not have been any more effective. Question—what is life's purpose, and what happens after I die? Answer—God has a purpose for everything and a plan for you and can offer you everlasting peace and happiness if you would only accept Jesus Christ as your Savior. Quite honestly, Martha was not even sure what that meant, but she knew for a fact that this surrender worked for her. She had found the answer, so there was no reason to torment herself with questions anymore. God said it through the Bible, I believe it, and that settles it! And it helped that this message was reinforced through constant repetition within her group.

All this was in place, and she felt it was effectively guiding her life until she came to Israel. *Ironic*, she thought. *I was a happy, content, unquestioning, born-again Christian until I came to the very place Jesus lived, and then the questioning started again.*

Actually, it was the betrayal by her preacher that ignited the initial questioning. And then there was the impact of actually seeing the places referenced in the Bible. When these places were set as images in her mind, they seemed big and magical and beautiful. When she saw them, however, they were not big. In fact, they were very small—the Via Dolorosa, Golgotha, Gethsemane, the Mount of Olives—they were not as she had imagined. They were close to one another and, by American standards, very small. The distance from Nazareth to Bethlehem was a few hours' car ride. And the Sea of Galilee was only a large lake, not much bigger than Florida's Lake Apopka and far smaller than Lake Okeechobee. And the river Jordon in places was not much more than what she would call a creek or branch in Florida. It made her realize that perhaps the writings in the Bible were authored by provincial thinkers whose world was quite limited and whose thoughts may have been restrained by this limitation. The great battles and struggles of that time were little more than minor local skirmishes by present-day standards.

It made her begin to question the legitimacy of the entire realm of Abrahamic religions. The one exception was Jesus himself. She had great love for this man who did not really ask for deification; he only asked people to be bold enough to totally commit to love and to peace. He was, to Martha, a true revolutionary, an ancient hippie whose message would not go away.

Martha's questioning was also promoted by the emotion evoked by the book her son had given her to read. She did not talk regularly with her son, for their relationship, while intact, still bore the scars of past struggles. He had been a bright child but was rebellious and resentful and was devastated by her second marriage. He eventually left her at about seventeen to live with his father—which did not work out too well either. He did manage to graduate from high school but did not pursue further education for about three years, during which time he led a chaotic life involving some drug and alcohol use and many minimum wage jobs.

Fortunately, he found a woman who recognized his potential and his goodness and who stood by him as he struggled through a painful period of adjustment. Now at age twenty-eight, he had become a functioning member of society, having gained a bachelors degree in science education and secured and maintained a position as a high school teacher with the Orange County, Florida, school district.

He eventually sought out his mother in a sincere effort to salvage their relationship, and this made her very happy. Her son had remained with the woman who had been so helpful. But they had not married, and there was no talk of having children. For Martha, it seemed a strange arrangement, but she realized she did not fully understand the thoughts and behavior of younger generations. She accepted things as they were and only hoped her son was happy.

While her son clearly enjoyed his reunion with his mother, he did not rejoice in her becoming a born-again Christian. He felt it repressed her intellect and kept her from exploring her own creativity. In fact, he felt his mother had always allowed others to define her life. Now it was the church and, of course, her latest husband—Phil. He had learned to ignore this man even though he detested him.

When he learned his mother was going to visit Israel and was going without Phil, he was hopeful. Perhaps things in Israel would awaken her spirit and allow her to spread her wings. He had called her with excitement and sent her a couple of books related to Israeli history, including *The Lemon Tree* by Sandy Tolan.

Martha began reading *The Lemon Tree* on the flight over and was about half-way through when she arrived in Tel Aviv. Once she landed in a hotel room, it took her about ten hours to shake off the jet lag. She awoke about 8:00 AM and, after having breakfast, met her group to begin their tour. It happened to be Saturday, which of course is the Sabbath, so few cars were on the road. This made the trip to Jerusalem quite enjoyable.

The road to Jerusalem was a well-constructed modern highway. However, she noticed that along the roadside were mangled, burned-out vehicles, which she was told by the tour director were purposely left as reminders of the 1948 struggles in establishing the Jewish state. While these were supposed to serve as monuments to the durability and determination of the Israeli people, Martha found them somewhat disturbing. In the United States, the violence of war was softened by enveloping the scars with green well-manicured parks. Yes, there were memorials and monuments but nothing that gave such raw evidence of the obscene violence. It was clear the Israeli culture viewed war differently. They did not shrink from its reality but, rather, reminded themselves of it with these grotesque artifacts—a blown-up truck, a piece of a downed aircraft. This kept them vigilant and aware. Martha knew she was in a different world. And as she continued reading *The Lemon Tree*, she began to realize that there was a complicated history behind the violence and hatred between the Jewish state and its Arab neighbors.

Strangely, however, Martha found herself invigorated by the culture of this region. There was conflict, which was always the aspect of the social dynamic that drew the attention of the media. But it appeared there were also compassion, cooperation, intelligence, awareness, and understanding.

What a paradox! Unmentionable violence and cruelty centered on the very location in which the world's greatest pacifist spoke of the power and greatness of love and forgiveness. It was perhaps the epicenter of the struggle between good and evil. But the lines between good and evil were not easily discerned. In the United States, it was made clear that Jews (i.e., the Israelis) were good, and the Arabs (i.e., the Palestinian Muslims) were evil. The lobbyists and the press, it appeared, made certain that this was the prevailing perception within the American public.

But Martha was quickly learning it was not that simple. As she visited the various religious sites around Jerusalem, she realized her interests were shifting away from the religious relics and ancient religious history and toward the nature of the more immediate struggles that permeated life in this region. In fact, she not only was becoming somewhat bored with the tour, she was often offended by the label "sacred," which was assigned to virtually every structure or site where someone had been buried or born or killed or arose into heaven or was built by some ancient leader or king. At the so-called Wailing Wall, when she saw grown men facing the wall, dressed in what looked like late nineteenth-century clothing, rocking back and forth, mumbling, talking and praying in whispers, and placing little notes into the cracks of the wall, she almost laughed out loud, which she knew would not be tolerated. In fact, as a woman, she could only approach the segregated women's section of the Wall and could not pray out loud near the main male section of the Wall. Martha found this not only silly but incongruent with the teachings of Jesus, whom she thought viewed all persons as equal in God's eyes. Was God really concerned about how people behaved around an ancient wall that was simply designed to hold up a building? It was, after all, made by people, not by God. Martha thought God, perhaps, would be more concerned about how people behaved around his creations—lakes and rivers and forests and deserts. These, however, were violated and destroyed without thought on a daily basis. Oddly enough, this was the first time she had mentally examined such things in this perspective. Israel was allowing her to think, and this thinking was exhilarating.

As they got back on the bus to go to Bethlehem, everyone was buzzing with excitement. They were going to actually see where

Jesus was born! But Martha withdrew from the group and continued reading the remaining pages of *The Lemon Tree*.

It was not a long ride to Bethlehem. It was planned that they would have lunch at a small café before continuing the tour. They were informed that Bethlehem was in Palestinian territory. There was no real danger, but people were reminded to be vigilant and stay with the group.

Wanting to continue her reading, Martha took a table by herself. After placing her order, she returned to the book and was immersed in its story when she heard a slightly accented male voice say, "I hope you are finding that book as interesting and thought provoking as I did. It is not the sort of thing we find many American tourists reading."

CHAPTER 7

I nitially, Martha was perturbed by this interruption. She slowly closed the book and looked up with the intent of delivering a terse response subtly laced with her irritation. What she saw, and what stopped her in midsentence, was a well-dressed, fit, late middle-aged man who looked to be a hybrid of Omar Sharif and Tom Selleck.

"I am not a typical American tourist" is what she wanted to say. Instead, it came out as, "I am not a typ—what about this book did you find so interesting?"

Martha had not been prepared for the feelings that were now trying to take over her being. She had not been attracted to someone in a romantic or sexual way for a long time, and yet, she was immediately taken by this man's presence. In truth, she could never remember being so attracted to anyone, at least, not on a first meeting. But it was not long before she gained her senses, and all the defense mechanisms began positioning themselves. This man, in all his attractiveness, was most likely a charlatan.

"Well, there are many things that make this an interesting book. But let's start with its honesty and complexity. May I sit down so I can explain?" he said.

"Uh, OK. But I am with a group, and I suspect we shall be leaving shortly," Martha said. Then she thought, *I sound like a smitten teenager. Why did I let this guy sit down? Be careful, Martha!*

"Thank you. My name is Khalil Suleiman. Literally, it means 'peaceful friend,' and I think you will find that it is a fitting name," he said with a slight smile.

Well, Martha doubted that, but she continued with her politeness. "I am Martha Browning, a simple American housewife from Indiana." She now was embarrassed by such a mundane introduction. She noticed several of her group companions were glancing suspiciously toward her table, which made her even more anxious. She also noticed he was wearing a wedding band.

"Do you know where Indiana is?"

He laughed. "I went to medical school at the University of Illinois—I am very familiar with Indiana!"

Oh God, she thought, *he is a doctor and educated in the US.* Not what she envisioned for the typical Palestinian Arab.

"You are Arab, aren't you, and Palestinian?" she said, again embarrassing herself with this hint of stereotyping.

"Well, I am Arab. But I am an Israeli citizen. I also, surreptitiously, consider myself Palestinian," he replied.

She knew from just her self-briefing about Israeli society that this was possible, even though most Americans were probably not aware of this possibility.

"And you are Muslim?" she said, deciding to continue her embarrassing questioning.

"Actually, I am Christian. At least, my family is Christian. And they have been for many generations. I am not as enthusiastic about religion as they are, however, which unfortunately caused my parents much anguish. But we have to follow our hearts, don't you think?"

An Arab-Israeli Christian doctor turned agnostic. This was almost more than Martha could comprehend. What would Phil think? She laughed silently just thinking of what kind of bigoted response might come out of his mouth.

"OK. You have gained my interest. Now tell me about why you find this book so intriguing, other than its honesty and complexity?" Martha said.

For the next few minutes, Khalil explained that he identified with a great deal of what was in the book because he had experienced much of what was discussed. His mother was pregnant with him when a number of those within the Arab community were forced to leave their homes to make way for the Jewish immigrants coming to establish a new Jewish state. He grew up seeing both hatred and kindness among all the groups as they struggled to find their place and their identity amidst the turmoil, violence, and chaos. He remembered the 1967 war and the mixed feelings he had regarding the expansion of the Israeli borders. He also recollected the humiliation and anxiety his family endured as an Arab-Christian family and the turbulence within the Orthodox Church as the role of Palestinians within the church was challenged and debated. Mostly, however, he remembered being among the children whose lives were deleteriously impacted by each of these conflicts, and he was particularly empathetic toward the Palestinian children who, through no fault of their own, became targets for violence, neglect, and abuse.

But he also told of his family's Jewish and Muslim friends and how friendships such as these had been formed, as long ago as the Ottoman Empire, during the rule of Suleiman the Magnificent—his family's namesake. He presented the Israeli-Palestinian dilemma in terms of a conflict not over religion but over greed and power enveloped in the convenient cloak of religion. It was through the financial and political help of his family's Jewish and Muslim friends, combined with his mother's and father's persistence, that Khalil was able to go to the United States to pursue a medical education. So he knew not to blame entire groups but, rather, dogma and specific fanatical individuals who impinged fear upon the masses and profited from the discontent and hatred. He praised Rabin and Peres but disliked Netanyahu and had a unique contempt for Sharon. Martha pretended to know who Sharon was and made a note to Google him when she got back to the hotel.

"Why are you in Bethlehem?" Martha asked.

"I give two days a week to help the orphanages and children's clinics, particularly within the Palestinian territory, as it is often difficult for them to access Israeli hospitals and clinics. On the Sabbath, I commit to the West Bank. Tomorrow I go to the Gaza Strip, which had suffered tremendously since the takeover by Hamas and imposition of the Israeli sanctions. One of the major West Bank clinics is close to Bethlehem, and I usually come here for lunch, if for no other reason than to watch the tourists," he responded. "Tomorrow, the real difficulty starts once I reach the Nahal Oz crossing between Israel and the Gaza Strip. Hopefully, I will not have to go to Karem Shalom to cross."

Noticing that Martha had been periodically glancing at his wedding band, he continued.

"My wife, who was a nurse, used to come with me, but she died two years ago of leukemia. I continue to wear this ring in respect for her. She was a wonderful wife and a dedicated mother, and I still miss her terribly. She was American, from Illinois. I met her while I was in medical school."

This last comment made Martha feel small and petty, for she knew he was aware of her curiosity regarding the ring. Finally, she commented, "I am married to a man named Phil who is back home in Indiana. He saw no reason to come to Israel."

"But you did? To come closer to Jesus, I presume?" he commented.

"Well, yes, at least initially," Martha continued. "Now I am wondering if there might be more to Israel than old religious sites and symbols. This book, *The Lemon Tree*, has awakened my thought process—thanks to my son, who told me I should read the book if I wanted to gain some insight into Israeli and Palestinian cultures."

Martha watched him closely as she made disclosure of her being married. Nothing about him changed, however—not a raising of eyebrows or a sigh of disappointment. She then told him in a whisper, so her companions could not hear, about the betrayal of her preacher, to which he laughed. He told her that was a common story. He noted, somewhat facetiously, that while Jesus was contemptuous of wealth, it appeared his self-appointed spokesmen, in many cases, considered wealth deserving payment for their devotion. He commented that such contradictions were plentiful in the world of institutionalized religious dogma. This was the main reason he separated from the church to pursue a life's philosophy based upon the actual teachings of Jesus and other revolutionaries associated with the development of Christianity, Islam, and Judaism, as well as other philosophies such as Taoism, Buddhism, and Zoroastrianism. He basically developed his own beliefs based upon a compilation of what he called the purest of these core beliefs, which had no need for tradition, protocol, or institutionalized worship rituals to confirm their legitimacy. Far from an agnostic, Khalil felt himself an enlightened worshipper of a forgiving, loving God who refused compartmentalization by human society and rejected the idea that any one group had sole ownership to truth, which served only to render other groups less holy, less deserving, and less valuable. If the Jews were God's chosen people, did that make him God's unchosen person? That did not feel very good, and he had trouble understanding why God would make such distinctions. His God didn't.

"But what about eternal life and the promise of heaven?" Martha said.

"I live my life with a healthy conscience, helping others as I can and expressing the truth as I perceive it. If that does not gain me passage into this Elysium, then so be it. And if conscious awareness ends with my dying and there is nothing after death, I can accept that also. I worry about what I can see and do in this life. The rest, I cannot control, so I give it little thought," he replied.

Noticing that her group was starting to gather outside the café, Khalil suggested it was time for her to go. He gave her a name of a small restaurant in Tel Aviv where he and a few friends were going to meet tomorrow night.

"It is probably near your hotel, so if you get a chance, come break bread with us," he said with a smile.

"I can't promise, but I will try. What time?" she replied.

"About 7:30 PM. Hope you can make it. Have a nice remainder of the day, Martha Browning."

"You too, Khalil Suleiman."

And then he was gone. She would make sure she would be there tomorrow night even though part of her told her it was not a good idea.

—ᴡᴏᴄᴏᴋᴏᴄᴋᴏᴏᴍ—

CHAPTER 8

—ᴡᴏᴄᴏᴄᴋᴏᴄᴋᴏᴏᴍ—

M artha found the tour of Bethlehem quite interesting. She learned that the site where it is said Jesus was born was a cave, not a manger. Martha wondered why a cave could not be a manger, but she did not think that argument was worth pursuing. As with the sites in Jerusalem, she felt the ceremony and the assignment of "sacred" was more about the event and the site than the person. Did it really matter where or how Jesus was born? She was not surprised it was a cave; it seemed there were a large number of caves in Israel, and they were used for everything—storage, habitat, raising pigeons and of course as hideouts. She could imagine Jesus and his group often hiding out in these caves—much like the representation that had been shown in the movie version of *Jesus Christ Superstar*.

It was becoming clear to Martha that her reaction to the Holy Land was much different than that of her companions. This surprised her as much as it did them. But what was most puzzling to her was that while she was experiencing a growing skepticism about the histrionics associated with religious institutions and the traditions they embraced, she felt she was actually gaining a greater understanding of Jesus, the social philosopher. She was not sure of the source of this understanding. Perhaps it had something to do with allowing herself to again engage in critical thinking and having the freedom to read a book given to her by her son—a book that Phil would probably not even allow in the house. It may have something to do with meeting a person like Khalil—a doctor who gave himself and his talents at no cost to help those who most needed the help. It also could be related to the underlying goodness that persisted in this mysterious land, even in the midst of violence and hatred. It was, she was certain, also linked to the harsh natural beauty of this region. Martha could envision Jesus meditating in the desert here, contemplating his fate, building his resolve to bring forward a bold message of pacifism and love.

All of this energized Martha, and she felt physically and emotionally strong and, for the first time in many years, really happy. And of course, she thought of Khalil, and she knew her exhilaration had much to do with the anticipation of seeing him tomorrow night.

The group finally arrived back in Tel Aviv about 5:00 PM. There was a planned dinner at a local restaurant that night, and while she was not enthused about attending, she did go. She enjoyed the food and the company and actually had a good time. But it was tomorrow night's dinner that was on her mind much of the time.

When they arrived back at the hotel, Martha asked the concierge about the restaurant Khalil had mentioned. He said it was just about three blocks away and, while small, was known for its excellent cuisine. It is local food, he said, and was not visited by that many American tourists. He asked her how she had found out about the restaurant. When she mentioned Khalil's name, the man's posture changed and he smiled brightly. "Dr. Suleiman is very well-known here—are you going to have dinner with him?"

"Well, I might, although I want to be sure it is safe. Based upon your reaction, I assume Dr. Suleiman can be trusted?" Martha asked.

"Without question!" the man said.

"Well, I suppose I shall go then. Please keep this conversation confidential. I think you understand why that is important," Martha said.

"Of course, of course," he said as Martha handed him five dollars. "And tell Dr. Suleiman that Amir says hello. He knows who I am."

"I will, Amir," she said, wondering how this man came to be so close to Khalil.

CHAPTER 9

The next day the group was up early. They were headed to the Sea of Galilee and Nazareth. They also were going to visit the site where Jesus delivered his Sermon on the Mount and, according to Matthew, issued the eight Beatitudes. These always puzzled Martha, and she wondered why her preacher did not discuss them in more detail in his sermons—particularly "Blessed are the meek, for they shall inherit the earth." She had asked him about this particular blessing, but his answer seemed meaningless and drifted off into explanations that the word *meek* may have been a mistranslation and that what Jesus was saying was that those who accept their station in life will inherit a stable social position. But to Martha, she felt that the *meek* were the patiently peaceful and the downtrodden. For example, the Africans, after years of persecution, were now becoming world leaders—Martin Luther King Jr., Nelson Mandela, Bishop Tutu, Kofi Anan, Colin Powell, Condoleezza Rice, John Lewis, and of course, Barack Obama. Were they inheriting the earth?

And then there was "Blessed are the pure of heart, for they shall see God" and "Blessed are the peacemakers, for they shall be children of God." If they were children of God, did that mean that Jesus was not the sole son of God? He apparently has a lot of peacemaker brothers and sisters. But this argument was discounted as silly by the preacher, and he would explain all this incongruity by exploring the theology of St. Augustine and Martin Luther and examining the myriad interpretations. When Martha suggested the statement was rather clear and why would people manipulate these words with interpretations that were molded to more closely represent what they wanted these Beatitudes to mean, her preacher would suggest, in a polite manner, that she was not trained in such complex theological matters and needed to be more receptive to and accepting of these interpretations and to his explanations.

But to Martha, it was clear; Jesus was a compassionate pacifist, and he believed that if society were to sincerely embrace pacifism and love, it would become stronger and more stable—"Among these, the greatest is love." To her, greatness meant power—love was power. His message was very revolutionary for the time, and it remains revolutionary today. And while Paul and Luke, among others, managed to convince much of the world to become followers of Christ, they did so by shifting the power of the Christian religion more toward the church structure and the promise of immortality and away from Jesus the philosopher. Jesus was the central image of the church, but his actual philosophy became occluded by the fascination of gaining eternal life by simply stating acceptance of Jesus as the earthly personification of the singular deity (God). Emulation of the philosophy of Jesus through deeds was not nearly as important as accepting Jesus as your Savior and, hence, receiving him as a conduit to eternal life. This is what Martha's preacher harped on week after week. There was no intellectual discussion of what "Turn the other cheek" meant, for example, which Martha interpreted as strong evidence of Jesus's pacifism. Rather, all the lectures and sermons invariably related to one's fate after death and the acceptance of Jesus into your heart—whatever that meant. After ten years of listening to this, Martha began to ask questions. This scared her, but it also excited her.

Martha listened quietly as they visited the various sites around Galilee. In a way, she was moved and fascinated, but she was certain her feelings were different than her companions, who reacted as they thought they should react. "I can feel the presence of the Lord," they would say, or "Now my acceptance of Jesus is complete." To Martha, this was just like drinking the Kool-Aid. While these visits seemed to answer questions for the others, for Martha, they served to generate new questions, and she felt, in fact, that this was healthy.

Thanks to a bus driver who ignored most of the rules of the road, the group arrived back at their hotel around 6:00 PM, somewhat shaken by the perilous bus ride. The group was again programmed to have supper together, but Martha simply said she did not feel like going. She did not mention her planned rendezvous with Khalil.

By 7:00 PM, the group was back on the bus, headed for a restaurant on the outskirts of Tel Aviv. Martha waited anxiously as the last person entered the bus. Then as the bus pulled out, she sighed with relief. She noticed that she was shaking slightly, and she took a deep breath in an effort to calm herself. By 7:15 PM, she was exiting the hotel, having given Amir a sly wink. Fortunately, no one from her group had stayed behind, so her departure was sufficiently clandestine.

Right at 7:30 PM, Martha walked into the restaurant. Khalil spotted her and waved her over to the table. He was wearing a light-blue silk shirt with gray slacks, which Martha thought accented his features perfectly. He was sitting with four others in a well-lit corner table. Martha was somewhat surprised that there were so many people, even though he had said he was meeting with some friends. She had envisioned perhaps just another couple. This looked more like a business meeting.

Khalil introduced his friends to Martha. There was David, Ali, Eliana, and Alex, and all were doctors and co-workers of Khalil's, except for David, who was a lawyer. Khalil explained that they all were members of a group trying to obtain more health-care access to Palestinian children. Right now, they were particularly concerned about the children in the Gaza Strip. Apparently, it had taken three hours today for Khalil to gain access to the Gaza Strip where he worked with active NGO doctors to care for the children victimized by the Israeli sanctions.

After some polite inquiries as to Martha's background and interests, the group got back to discussing the issue of Palestinian health-care access. Martha found out that both David and Ali had attended school in the United States, and that Ali had received his medical degree from the University of Florida, which was Martha's alma mater as well. The brief exchange of Gatorology made her feel a bit more comfortable.

At some point, she asked if the work they were doing was being monitored by the Israeli authorities. Khalil laughed and said, "Of course, why do you think I spent three hours at the border crossing today?"

This scared Martha somewhat. "You don't think they will investigate me just because I am meeting with you?"

David smiled at her before commenting, "This is a democracy, and I can assure you that harassing American tourists is not something that is encouraged. They know what you are doing, but it will not raise any red flags—but do not try to go to Gaza! And when you leave, they will possibly quiz you at the airport. Tell them everything regarding your comings and goings while you were in Israel. Do not lie about anything—they are well trained to detect lies."

This explanation did not make Martha feel that much better, but she had already decided to not shirk from such things. She simply thanked David and continued listening.

During the course of their meeting, Martha gained an admiration for their dedication and commitment. And while it was not discussed, she knew each of them was taking a risk in advancing their agenda. Here was a group that included men and women—Jews, Christians, Muslims, Arabs, and Hebrews—joined by the very philosophy promoted by Jesus: love, compassion, and peace. They did not need to do this. *Yes*, she thought, *this is where Jesus becomes real.* He is revealed as a bold revolutionary who said, "Blessed are those who are persecuted for the sake of righteousness, for theirs is the Kingdom of Heaven." This group gave real meaning to this Beatitude. If ever Martha had been in the presence of Jesus, it was tonight with these dedicated people. Her trip to the Holy Land was indeed bringing her closer to Jesus, just not in the way she expected.

CHAPTER 10

Martha, at age twenty-six, finally came to realize that she was an attractive woman. Before that, even though others had told her of her beauty, she could not believe them. But at twenty-six, just after the end of her first marriage, she became convinced that men found her very appealing. This she viewed as both a curse and a blessing. She had learned that when a woman is attractive, doors open, but often for the wrong reasons. Any display of competence or intelligence, Martha found, was often seen by men as bothersome and an inconvenience that was quickly discounted.

Now in her fifties, Martha was thankful that while she was still attractive, her age allowed her to usually avoid confrontation with the more base mating displays so characteristic of hormone-driven young men. Older men did often give her a second glance, but they were easier to manage, and their intent was typically more complex than just sex. Martha had kept her body trim over the years, thanks to a balanced diet and a morning exercise routine, so she did look younger than her age, and it was not uncommon for men to look and, at times, make advances, regardless of their age. But she could tell what they wanted, and she typically would dismiss them as shallow and self-absorbed.

But Khalil was different. He was at least her age, probably a few years older, but he was stunning in his mannerisms and his appearance. He was a man that did not need to pursue women, for they would pursue him. And as she listened to him talk, she knew he was a serious thinker and a compassionate person. He was not one to trivialize romantic love, nor was the tallying of sexual conquests part of his repertoire. Love was important, in fact, too important, to be viewed so casually. She was, she knew, falling in love with him, which was problematic because she was married—not happily married, but married nonetheless. Martha did not come to Israel to cheat on her husband. But she did want to spend more time with this man.

And then a question came into her mind. Why did Khalil approach her? She felt it was not just to pursue a seduction. There were many American women in Israel her age, or younger, who were easier, more attractive targets for this sort of game. And he certainly did not need her money, for she was not wealthy and, in fact, was likely less so than he. Did she remind him of his deceased wife? Was there some surreptitious role he saw for her that involved some intrigue related to his traveling between Israel and the Palestinian territory? Maybe it really was the book that caught his attention. It was enigmatic. Perhaps things would become clearer as they spent time together.

As Martha listened to the group's conversation, she began to comprehend even more fully the complexity of the Palestinian issue. Underlying all the mistrust, suspicion, fear, and political maneuvering was a confusing bureaucratic component that added an additional layer of obstruction. While many looked at Khalil's group as heroes, others apparently were suspicious of their motives. They could be spies for either side, or they could be using their humanitarian goals as a front for more pernicious purposes. No question, they were watched closely by all sides.

The assassination of Rabin more than a decade and a half earlier had sent a clear message that not only were there Jewish groups opposed to any compromise regarding Jewish encroachment into Palestinian lands but also that some within these groups were quite dangerous. On the Palestinian side, particularly some aligned with Hamas, there had been displayed a propensity for violence. It was indeed a volatile situation, and while it was quite obvious to Martha that Khalil and his friends were solely concerned about the children, she knew that they were exposing themselves to danger from both extremes. *This was so different from Indiana,* she thought. Complacency, which was a constant companion in Indiana and one she had welcomed freely into her life, was rare in Israel and nonexistent within this particular group.

Between extended, complicated conversations and the long wait for their food order, it was past 10:00 PM before they finally left the restaurant. Khalil insisted on walking Martha to her hotel. On the walk back, she asked him if he knew an Amir. He said he knew several people named Amir. She asked then if he knew an Amir who worked as the concierge at her hotel. This caused him to stop and to smile.

"Yes, I know who you are talking about. I took care of his younger half-brother. He comes from a wonderful family. Please tell him hello for me," he said.

"What was wrong with his brother?" Martha asked.

"Well, to start off, he was stuck in Gaza City," noted Khalil. "And considering he had a bad heart valve, things were not looking too good. David, Ali, and I worked very hard to get him the surgery he needed in an Israeli hospital. He is doing quite well now although he had to go back to Gaza City. I see him occasionally when I am there. He is a fine young man, but he is in an unsafe environment and is vulnerable to being influenced by radicals."

Martha noticed he was getting somewhat emotional, and she placed her hand on his arm in a gesture of understanding.

"I am new to such things. We hear about the difficulties in Gaza back home, but quite honestly, we do not give it much thought. We are saturated with stories like these—Sudan, Burma, North Korea, Somalia, Syria. The result is a general ambivalence. We can make them go away by simply changing TV channels. We are so comfortable and have so much, it is difficult for us to understand these situations. We do give, and our government does get involved, but I suppose we do not sense the urgency," Martha said.

"I know," Khalil said, "there will always be poor—as Jesus said. All anyone can do is love and give."

Martha felt helpless—sure, she could give some money, but was she willing to give up her comfort and affluence for these causes? Honestly, it did not have much appeal, and Khalil did not push her into facing these realities. They said little during the remainder of their walk. At the hotel, Martha said good-bye to Khalil and thanked him for a nice evening. He smiled and turned to walk away but stopped after a few steps and turned toward her.

"Martha," he said, trying to get her attention.

"Yes?" she answered as she turned to face him.

"When is your tour over?" he asked.

"Tuesday, why?"

"And when do you fly back"

"Wednesday morning"

"Well, I am going to Haifa Wednesday to see some friends and visit a small clinic there and, of course, relax a little and hike around Mount Carmel. It is an enchanting place. Do you think you could change your flight by a couple of days and come with me?"

Martha was stunned. "Well, this is something I will have to think about. Call me late Tuesday afternoon, and I will let you know."

Martha immediately began thinking about how to arrange this. She would have to call Phil and tell him she came upon an opportunity to visit other parts of Israeli and would be staying for a couple more days. She knew he would grumble, but she also knew he was probably enjoying himself in her absence and would not be too upset. Next, she had to change her flight. The hotel could help her with that probably. And then there was the issue of her group. *Well, she thought, it is none of their business*. She knew the rumors would blossom, but she would just have to deal with that later. Martha realized she had already decided to go to Haifa.

CHAPTER 11

On Monday, the group visited Masada and the Dead Sea. They also had planned to go to Jericho, but Israeli security had strongly advised against it. This turned out for the better because they got to spend extra time at Masada. Martha was fascinated by this place. Not so much over the history as over its massive physical presence. While things in the cities seemed so small, Masada, the Judas Desert, and the Dead Sea seemed bigger than life and so strange when compared to Indiana or Florida. For some reason, Martha was totally enchanted by this entire landscape. And of course, she got to bathe in the Dead Sea and coat herself with the mud that was said to be so rejuvenating. It was great fun, and when she arrived back in the hotel, she was exhausted.

After taking a shower, she came back down to the hotel to see if they had been able to change her flight. They said it was no problem, and the lady behind the desk handed her the revised flight—Friday at 11:00 AM. That was perfect!

While Martha was putting her ticket in her purse, she noticed two ladies from her group in the lobby. They saw her and asked if she wanted to have dinner with them. She said sure, and the three of them walked out to grab a taxi.

The restaurant the two ladies had chosen was OK but not as authentic as the one she had eaten at the night before. The food was Middle Eastern but modified to be more American. It was, however, enjoyable to sit and relax and talk about today's tour. Martha, however, did not mention her change in plans. She would save that for a later time.

When she got back to the hotel, it was only 9:00 PM, which meant it was 2:00 PM in Indiana. She knew Phil did not work on Mondays, so she called him to discuss her new plan. The conversation was a bit painful and tedious, but in the end, all was well. He would pick her up at the airport at the new time. Now all that was left was to wait for Khalil's call tomorrow.

CHAPTER 12

Martha woke up early Tuesday morning with a case of serious anxiety about her plans to spend time with Khalil. Some of it had to do with Phil. While she had not lied to him, she did withhold details—not that he asked for any. However, her anxiety had a great deal more to do with her inability to control her feelings toward Khalil. He was, in her eyes, the perfect man, and that scared her. At her age, she was not sure she could deal with a perfect man in her life. In a way, it was more comfortable to be with someone like Phil, someone who did not excite her spirit, someone who made complacency and ambivalence easy to accept.

Of course, there was a time when she had thought Phil was the perfect man. Only later did she come to realize that this perfect man was not him but the image he built around himself. And he sustained the illusion of this image for quite some time.

Martha met Phil at a time of transition in her life. She had come to realize and admit that she was an alcoholic, a lover of Wild Turkey, straight up—a traditional Southern drink. When the Turkey was scarce, she would settle for large quantities of beer or really cheap whiskey. She went through the AA routine and came out sober but not totally fixed emotionally. That was when she turned to the church. A friend from AA introduced Martha to her preacher, and soon, he was also her preacher. Martha embraced the church and the born-again sales pitch with unbridled enthusiasm. It was just what she needed at that time, she felt. She made friends, attended prayer meetings, listened to sermons, went to Bible study—she was at the church almost every night. And this was when she met Phil.

Phil was about her age—in his forties at that time. He had been married once before. His wife divorced him after she ran off with an office associate. She left him with two teenage children—a boy, fourteen, and a girl, seventeen. He and his wife had been college sweethearts—he being on the track team, she being a cheerleader. They were the quintessential American couple for about seven years. Then she started serious drinking, and it went downhill from there.

Phil was an accountant—not an exciting career but stable and reliable. But what impressed Martha the most was how he loved and cared for his two kids. Unlike most men, Phil abhorred alcohol—at least, that was the picture he painted for Martha. He played the poor, pitiful victim convincingly. And he was attractive in an athletic sort of way and was loyal to the church and, like Martha, was a born-again Christian. They dated for about a year before getting married. By this time, his daughter was in college, so only the boy was at home. This was Martha's third marriage, and she was determined it would be her last.

Martha's son had left her to go live with his father shortly after she started dating Phil. To compensate for her son leaving, she doted on Phil's son, and they became quite close. In fact, they remained close. He was an excellent student and ended up in veterinary school. He just recently started his own practice in Louisiana, of all places. His new wife was from an old family from northern Louisiana, so he started off his practice well positioned in the community. He seemed happy, and she wished him the best.

Phil's daughter was another case altogether. Much like Martha's son, she was rebellious. However, unlike her son, she never changed. When Martha and Phil got married, she quit college and hooked up with a so-called musician—although he had very little talent. Of course, there were drugs and an abortion and bailing out of jail. Almost predictably, she eventually moved back with Martha and Phil when the pseudo-musician went foraging in greener pastures. And Phil enabled her, which made things worse. But when Martha would try to intervene, she felt his wrath. The loving, gentle Phil disappeared.

The fact was, Phil was very controlling, and Martha recognized that he was probably always controlling. He wanted Martha to follow certain regimens—when to have supper, what was allowable and not allowable for supper, when to go to bed, when to wake up, even what clothes to wear, what to say at their parties, and who she could have as friends. In addition, it was becoming evident also that Phil was a bigot—and not a low-key bigot. He had names for everyone who was not a white male Protestant, often vulgar names, particularly when referring to women. After five years of marriage, Martha knew she had made another mistake.

Eventually, Phil and Martha reached a stalemate. Phil spent time with his male friends and started drinking beer and going to sports bars. And while Martha remained very active with the congregation, he had given up on the church. He said he was still Christian but did not like the people at church. And he spent a great deal of money on his daughter, who continued to exploit his enabling tendencies. Every month it was something different—beauty school, singing lessons, computer technician, respiratory technician. She even spent two months with her brother, helping him as she trained to be a veterinary technician. He and his wife kicked her out of the house when they caught her snorting cocaine off their expensive glass coffee table. And of course, she came back to Phil, who immediately signed her up in classes to be an environmental technician. That lasted two weeks.

Oddly enough, Martha loved this girl and was sad to see her struggle so. She was self-deluded and did not seem capable of putting forth a real effort toward anything. Martha was convinced that as long as Phil was there, she never would confront herself or seek some degree of self-realization. It was a sad situation, and she was not sure what, if anything, she could do to help.

About four months before Martha left for Israel, Phil's daughter moved into an apartment with her new boyfriend. Martha actually liked this guy, and she hoped perhaps he could help guide her toward a normal life, much in the way her son's girlfriend had guided him. She prayed very hard for her stepdaughter and was encouraged when the relationship appeared to be going strong after two months. But Phil was determined to destroy his daughter's relationship with this man—partly because he was mixed white and African American and partly because Phil was jealous, although he would never admit that.

Martha knew Phil fed upon his daughter's dependency upon him, and the extent of this dysfunction became even more evident to Martha as Phil orchestrated a deceptive manipulation of his daughter, which eventually resulted in her terminating her relationship with this new boyfriend.

"I knew he was no good. Being half-nigger, he had to be worthless. If she would have stayed with him, he would have eventually beaten her. He would get drunk and come home and beat the crap out of her. I am glad she saw what he was before she got hurt," Phil exclaimed.

Phil had told his daughter that he had seen her boyfriend in a bar with a black girl—he used the term *nigger bitch*. Even though the girl turned out to be his half-sister, Phil's daughter did not believe this, even when her boyfriend brought his half-sister to their apartment to introduce her.

So thanks to Phil, when Martha left for Israel, her stepdaughter was back in their house. Perversely, this made Phil happy. Martha began to think seriously about asking for a divorce, but she held off, hoping that perhaps this trip would provide some answers and allow her to discover an alternative strategy.

After being in Israel for several days, Martha began to more clearly understand this situation. Phil was, in a dysfunctional way, seeking to establish a position of respect and dominance within his family group. He desired to be that patriarch upon whom their very safety and welfare was dependent. The problem, however, is that there was a paucity of authentic physical threats in Indiana. Phil did not provide sustenance as an accomplished farmer or hunter, nor did he fend off physical threats from other males with his superior fighting skills or his mental acumen. The one thing he could do, however, was provide money to attempt to resolve difficult situations. This worked very well when his children were small and totally dependent upon him. But once they became adults, there was a real threat that they would become independent and fully capable of resolving their own problems. This was exactly what his son did, but his daughter was a more vulnerable target. It did not take much for him to sustain her dependency upon him and thereby allowing him to remain as the nurturing and protective patriarch.

Of course, in a more volatile and treacherous social dynamic such as that in much of the Middle East, it is easier for this patriarchal hero impulse to find legitimacy. And in a strange twist, these stresses appeared to often stabilize the family and make life's purpose clearer. Khalil's status, for example, as a strong, protective patriarch would never be in question. Martha wondered how much of America's challenges related to mental illness found genesis in this thesis. Perhaps our life is too easy and the absence of physical and intellectual challenges is actually damaging to the human psyche.

And then she thought of Jesus and his disciples struggling to endure the harsh Israeli environment while dodging the prejudices and institutional condemnation associated with the social dynamic of that time. She thought of the tremendous strength it took to face the paradigm of prejudice, violence, and lethal punishment in order to preach love, forgiveness, and pacifism and then to endure the physical pain of prosecution because of a refusal to abandon these beliefs. This was the essence of courage.

Martha recognized that just as Americans refused to face the raw ugliness of war, they also refused to seriously confront the reality associated with suffering such as that experienced by Jesus. Like the war memorials and monuments softened by trees and manicured lawns, the brutality of crucifixion was obscured by beautiful churches, soothing music, and invented voices intended to project solemnity delivered by preachers with soft hands, coiffured hair, and dressed in $2,000 silk suits. And yes, the preachers did talk about the suffering of Jesus, but it never seemed that real or that convincing when set in such tranquil, opulent backdrops.

In America, when unemployment increases to over 8 percent and there is talk of widespread suffering, you would think the country was entering a period of a black plague epidemic and widespread famine. It was labeled a tragedy when people had to give up cable television and cut back to two six-packs a week in order to balance their budgets or their kids actually had to work to help pay for their college education.

But there was real suffering in the Middle East. Martha could feel it and could see its impact. Khalil saw it his whole life. It was part of the social fabric, and confronting it and trying to attenuate its influence gave character and strength to the people.

CHAPTER 13

After breakfast, Martha and her group loaded onto the bus for a quick ride to a small building in Tel Aviv. Here they met a panel of Christian historians who lectured for about two hours about the importance of the sites they had visited in the development of Christianity. It was interesting but became somewhat repetitious toward the end. Eventually, the session was completed, and the group walked a few blocks to a small restaurant to have lunch. Martha noticed her preacher was there, greeting each person in the group. She did not think he knew that she was aware of his profiteering and that was verified when he approached her and asked with a smile if the tour had met her expectations. Martha did not feel like a confrontation, so she smiled quickly and said it had been very uplifting.

By 1:00 PM, Martha was getting rather anxious as she expected Khalil would call her as early as 2:00 PM. She wanted to be in her room by then. Fortunately, lunch wrapped up by 1:15 PM, and it was not long before she was sitting by her bed, waiting.

While she waited, she finished the last few pages of *The Lemon Tree*. The book was sad, in a way, but very enlightening. She would have to remember to thank her son for giving it to her.

Finally, at 3:15 PM, the room phone rang. She answered it and heard Khalil's voice.

"Have you decided about the trip to Haifa?" he asked.

"Yes, I want to go," she answered.

"Excellent. I shall pick you up at the hotel at 10:00 AM."

"That works. My group is leaving for the airport at 8:00 AM."

"Until then, and be sure you bring a warm jacket and some walking shoes."

After the conversation, Martha called the lady in charge of coordinating the group, informing her that she would be staying in Israel until Friday and had already changed her ticket. The lady was initially confused, asking if anything was wrong. Martha informed her that she had an opportunity to visit other parts of Israel.

"You understand the tour cannot assume any responsibility for anything that happens once you decide not to take tomorrow's flight?" she said.

"Yes, I understand," answered Martha.

"OK, then. Have fun, but be careful. We will see you back in Indiana."

It was done. Martha decided to have just a simple meal in the hotel, pack, and get to bed early. Tomorrow, she imagined, would be a real adventure. She was proud of herself for grasping this opportunity.

CHAPTER 14

K halil showed up right at 10:00 AM in a red Renault Clio. As most of the cars in Tel Aviv, she noticed, were white, Khalil's car really stood out. Martha greeted him as he helped place her luggage in the car. Soon they were headed toward Haifa.

"I am so glad you decided to come with me," Khalil said. "We are going to spend the night at my daughter's home. Her name is Salem. She is married and has one small child—a girl named Dahlia. Her husband, Nadim, teaches at the University of Haifa. We are going to stop at the university first and will hike the trails around the Carmel Mountains. It will take less than two hours to get there, unless the traffic is really bad. I packed us a small lunch for our hike."

For the next hour, they travelled northward along the Mediterranean coast toward Haifa. Fortunately, the traffic was not bad, so it looked as though they would be able to keep Khalil's schedule. Khalil would frequently comment about certain landmarks, often embellishing his comments with personal experiences—a family vacation, camping trips with schoolmates, his first job as a young teenager, swimming in the sea with his baby daughter. Martha was impressed at his knowledge not only of the landscape and the history but also the ecology. He was familiar with the plants and flowers and the myriad of indigenous birds and animals. He knew which plants and fruits were edible or medicinal or poisonous. She envisioned Khalil as a young boy, spending hours exploring the coast and the hills of Israel.

And of course, there were old fortresses built by the Crusaders and remnants of the Romans such as the aqueducts. For each of these, there was an associated fascinating story. Martha was mesmerized.

After about an hour and a half, they reached the university. Khalil called his son-in-law on his cell phone and asked him to meet them in a certain parking lot. Nadim was waiting when they pulled up. He was a slender man, probably early forties. He looked healthy but not athletic—a true academic. Martha found his smile charming, and she noticed he was attractive in what her son would call a "nerdy" sort of way.

Martha could tell that Nadim and Khalil were close by the way they interacted. They greeted each other with an embrace, and Khalil kissed him lightly on the cheek.

"Nadim, this is Martha. She is a friend I met in Bethlehem."

Nadim responded politely, "It is so nice to meet you, Martha. I hope you will enjoy your stay with us. I believe my wife has a special meal planned tonight although I am not supposed to know that."

"I look forward to it," Martha replied. "I think before we leave for your house, however, Khalil is going to show me around some of the trails here. Is he a good tour guide?"

"The best in Israel," Nadim said with a smile. "You need to take notes if you expect to remember everything he tells you."

"Well. OK, then, let's go! See you tonight, Nadim, and very nice meeting you."

As they turned to leave, Martha noticed that Nadim whispered something to Khalil, who responded with a nod and a smile.

"What was that about?" asked Martha.

"Nothing, he just said he liked you," Khalil responded.

"That is strange, he just met me. I might actually be a monster," Martha said jokingly.

In a manner that Martha found shockingly serious, Khalil whispered, "Nadim has seen real monsters. Trust me, he is a good judge of character."

Martha decided to let this comment drop. Obviously, ugly things happen in this region from time to time, and she did not want that ugliness to interfere with the happiness of this moment. They could talk about such things later. Khalil sensed her concern and did not pursue the issue further.

CHAPTER 15

For about an hour, they walked along a well-worn trail. Martha was amazed at how wild some of the vistas appeared. It was considerably different than the desert but still very impressive. It reminded her somewhat of the California chaparral although a bit more lush. It was clear to Martha that Khalil had visited these hills many times before, and as they walked, he would at times take diversions along small pathways to show her special plants or hidden vistas.

Once they came across a group of rock hyrax, a small animal that looked to Martha like a strange mixture of rabbit and groundhog. Fortunately, Khalil saw the group before they saw him. Once they became aware of Khalil and Martha's presence, they made a shrill alarm sound and quickly disappeared into the rocks.

Martha was thankful that it was springtime, for the hills were blanketed in myriad wild flowers. This attracted a number of birds, including the Palestinian sunbird, which Martha had come to admire since arriving in Israel, and a very colorful little bird that Khalil called a bee-eater.

After hiking a rather steep slope, they arrived at the top of a hill, which allowed them to look to the west over the Mediterranean. Here they stopped for lunch. Khalil had prepared baba ghanouj and hummus with pita bread and a few dates and figs for dessert. After lunch, Khalil volunteered a brief history of Nadim's experiences as a young Maronite Christian in Lebanon during that country's bloody civil war of the seventies and eighties.

As Khalil described all the groups involved in the war, Martha again was reminded of the complexity of the Middle East. In spite of Khalil's effort to present facts in the simplest terms possible, Martha still had trouble grasping the cause and nature of the alliances and conflicts among these groups, which included Maronite Christians, Druze, Israelis, Syrians, the Palestinian Liberation Organization (PLO), Sunni Muslims, Shia Muslims, and Hezbollah, as well as external involvement by the United States and other countries. In addition, within many of these groups, there were divisions. For example, some Maronites aligned themselves with the Israelis while a few favored the PLO. It did seem apparent to her, however, that much of the tension found genesis in the Palestinian refugee situation, which she felt was correlated with the creation of the new Israeli State.

Khalil explained that Nadim was about five years old when the conflict began and was twelve when rogue members of the Maronite militia known as Phalangists massacred well over a thousand Palestinians and Lebanese in the Sabra and Shatila refugee camps in 1982. Indications were that the massacre was conducted with Israeli involvement although whether this was direct or indirect is still questioned by many. The Israeli commander at that time was Ariel Sharon.

Nadim's father was not a supporter of the Phalangists even though he was Maronite, and he was openly critical of the Israeli involvement and particularly contemptuous of Sharon. Three weeks after the massacre, Nadim's home was attacked and his mother and father killed. Nadim escaped only because he was not at home during the attack, having not yet returned from a summer's stay with his uncle in Haifa. Who exactly was responsible was never determined although most felt it was likely someone who did not appreciate Nadim's father's criticisms. Nadim's uncle immediately moved his family, along with Nadim, to a safer part of Haifa. He and his wife, with their two other children, reared Nadim and even helped finance his higher education. It was too dangerous for Nadim to return to Lebanon during the war, and he was not able to even attend his parent's funeral. After the war, Nadim did return and was able to visit his parent's gravesite.

During his public school years, Nadim excelled as a student and developed rapidly into a true intellect. He attended university in Israel and was eventually able to gain acceptance at Oxford where he completed his doctorate in international relations.

For reasons that Khalil even had trouble understanding at times, Nadim did not seek or desire revenge for the murder of his father and mother. Instead, he became an ardent pacifist and an open critic of institutionalized religion. He became fascinated with game theory and evolutionary biology, particularly as they relate to the role of cooperation and altruism, both in the evolution of human societies and the evolution of the human species itself. While at Oxford, he attended several lectures by Richard Dawkins and became even more enthralled with his theory of the selfish gene.

Martha interrupted Khalil at the mention of Dawkins.

"This is the same guy who wrote *The God Delusion*? He is an atheist—our preacher talks about him as if he were the Antichrist!" Martha said in dismay.

"Well, he presents himself as a qualified or second-level atheist, stating that there is no scientific evidence for the existence of the Abrahamic God often called Yahweh, Jehovah, or Allah, and that it makes little sense to establish institutional worship around an unsubstantiated deity. He also notes that he has no conclusive evidence that this Yahweh does not exist, just as no one could provide evidence of the nonexistence of a Flying Spaghetti Monster—as fabricated by Dawkins himself. I believe he is a little harsh in his criticism at times, as does Nadim. On the other hand, he finds himself intellectually connected to the living earth, so it would be unfair to state that Dawkins has no belief system, it is just based upon scientific evidence," Khalil answered.

"Well, I will admit that I have been indoctrinated to not like this guy very much," Martha replied. "But in all fairness, I have not read anything he has written."

"But you trust your preacher, right?" Khalil said somewhat sarcastically.

"Well, I did at one time but, now, not so much," Martha noted.

"Well, I am sure you will find Nadim's conversation interesting tonight."

Martha did not like confrontation and chose not to allow their discussion to evolve into an argument. Rather, she changed the subject, asking about the name of a small flower she noticed next to the path. Khalil got the hint—he also was not anxious to get into verbal combat with Martha—at least, not yet.

As they walked back to the parking lot, they said very little. However, once in the car, Martha smiled and quietly thanked Khalil for inviting her to come with him and for sharing the walk with her. He smiled at her and nodded a "you're welcome" as they continued their drive toward Haifa.

CHAPTER 16

From the university, it took less than half an hour for Khalil to drive to his daughter's home in a section of Haifa known as Wadi Nisnas, which Khalil said with a chuckle was named for the mongoose. Martha had never experienced anything quite like Wadi Nisnas—the narrow streets, the marketplace, the smells of bread and spices, painted walls and religious symbols, and the stone houses, with arched windows and balconies, all crowded against one another in an asymmetric fashion. She found it enchanting and yet chaotic at the same time.

As they wound through the narrow streets, Khalil explained, without being apologetic, that his daughter's house was humble by American standards. It was located in a crowded but friendly neighborhood. He said the atmosphere of Wadi Nisnas was reminiscent of Arab towns of much earlier periods, which Martha took to mean pre-1948. The neighbors included Jews, Arab, Christians, Muslims, and a few Druze, and everyone got along fairly well although, at times, one could sense underlying prejudices. The Jewish community made a real distinction between the term

Palestinian and *Arab*. They generally thought of people like Khalil as Arab Israeli, not Palestinian Israeli, while the Arab community quite often preferred the term *Palestinian*, which at times could be irritating to some in the Jewish community.

Khalil explained that his daughter's house actually belonged to Nadim as he had inherited it from his uncle, who had served as his father for much of his life. His uncle owned several houses in Haifa, and through his will, distributed them to his own two children and to Nadim. While he was still living, one of Nadim's uncle's houses had been leveled to make room for an Israeli project without much compensation being offered by the Israeli government. This was an all-too-common practice that had understandably caused consternation among the Arab community. With Nadim's help, and the help of a Jewish Israeli lawyer who was a classmate of Nadim's at Oxford, his uncle was eventually able to gain some reasonable amount of compensation through the courts.

For Martha, it was hard to comprehend such disregard for private property. In the United States, while governments could indeed be heavy-handed regarding the taking of property, they were restrained by the courts and the laws of eminent domain. While the American public regularly complained about too much government in their lives, they often forgot that such checks and balances within the government served their interests. She thought it must take great patience and understanding to be non-Jewish in Israel. Ironically, however, she was learning that some of the closest allies to the non-Jewish citizens were secular Israeli Jews. She was finally starting to gain some grasp of the complex dynamics of this region of the world.

About five minutes after entering the Wadi Nisnas neighborhood, Khalil pulled the car into a small archway next to a two-story home close to an intersection. Before he could get to the front door, a young girl came running out of the house, arms open, screaming "Giddo, Giddo!"

Khalil knelt down and took the girl in his arms and, in English, replied, "Dahlia, you sweet angel! Say hello to my friend Martha."

"Hello, Martha," Dahlia said as she turned to Martha, holding out her hand. Her English was heavily accented and spoken slowly, as if she had to pull the words from a memorization list. Martha noticed that the girl, who was perhaps six years old, was indeed angelic in appearance. She had light-brown hair at shoulder length and green eyes, with light olive-colored skin and an infectious smile and, of course, an abundance of energy.

"She is learning English and is a quick student. She speaks Arabic as her main language but is also pretty good in Hebrew," Khalil remarked. Then turning to Dahlia, in English, he said, "Take Martha upstairs to meet your mother."

Dahlia grabbed Martha's hand and pulled her through the door up the stairs. "Momma, Momma, come see Martha!" she said in English.

As Martha approached the top of the stairs, she saw a slim young woman smiling at them. When the woman saw Martha, she threw one hand over her mouth in surprise and muttered, "Oh my goodness, Martha, you are my mother's twin!" This answered Martha's question regarding Khalil's interest in her. The woman embraced Martha, holding back tears. "It is so nice to meet you, Martha. I am Salem. Come here and let me show you a picture of my mother!"

Salem led Martha to a small alcove, which served solely as a family picture room. There were a few old black-and-white photos of circa early twentieth century, which were obviously of family patriarchs and matriarchs—Khalil's father, Nadim's father and mother, Nadim's uncle, etc. Most of the other photographs were in color. One of the larger pictures was of a woman, perhaps forty years old, with auburn-colored hair, blue eyes, and a hint of vestigial freckles. This was Khalil's wife, Salem's mother. Martha thought that this woman could be her sister; the resemblance was that close.

"We do favor, don't we?" Martha replied, using an old Southern expression for noting similarities in appearance. Salem smiled, still noticeably shaken. It was clear to Martha she did not totally understand this colloquialism, so she explained. "That is to say, we do look alike."

"Yes, yes!" Salem replied. "Pardon me if I seem surprised, my father told me about you but did not say you looked like mother. It is wonderful, of course. Are you of Scottish descent as my mother was?"

Martha laughed. "I am, like millions of others in America. Of course, there is some Native American and Irish and Italian and Polish mixed in there as well and, most likely, a trace of African. We Americans are all hybrids—or mongrels—depending how you wish to see us."

"I like hybrid, for that's what I am also. My father and my husband are pure Arab but not me and not Dahlia. I like to think we add some spice to their conservative natures!" Salem said, smiling. Martha could see that was true, for Salem had fair skin and greenish-blue eyes that gave away her mixed heritage. She also had a sparkle in her eyes that Martha found very appealing. She loved Salem immediately. She was so glad she had decided to come to Haifa!

"You know, I must make a correction. While I say my husband is pure Arab, he prefers to call himself Phoenician, which makes me laugh, for the Phoenicians were great sailors and navigators. Nadim gets seasick just looking at the ocean!" Salem giggled. "Here, let me pour you some Arabic tea—it is quite delicious. My father should be up shortly. Oh, here he comes now."

"Looks like you ladies have found each other. Noor, could you please pour me some tea?" Khalil said, after giving Salem a kiss and hug.

"He calls me Noor sometimes, just as a kind of nickname. It means 'light,'" Salem remarked to Martha as she poured her father some tea. Then turning to Khalil, she said in a mocking scowl, "You did not tell me Martha looked so much like Mother—I almost fell down the stairs when I saw her."

"Just a little surprise. You know Martha lives in Indiana—near Bloomington didn't you say?" he asked, glancing over to Martha. "My wife, Sara, was reared on a farm near Vincennes, on the Illinois side of the Wabash River. When I first saw the farmland in that area, I was overwhelmed. America is blessed with an abundance of agriculture. Anyway, I was so nervous when I first met her parents—I was afraid they would not like their daughter dating an Arab. But you know, they were the most gracious people—and remained that way until the day they died—God rest their souls."

"I remember them quite well, they were wonderful," Salem said, selecting a picture from the collection to show Martha. "You know, I was born in America, and even after we moved back to Israel, I would often spend a couple of weeks with my mother during the summers on their farm. I absolutely loved it—although they made us work hard! Martha—you probably know what I am talking about if you are from Indiana?"

Martha laughed. "Not hardly, I was born and reared in north-central Florida. We had farms around us but not the size of those in the Midwest. Many of our neighbors in rural areas raised pigs—probably not a lot of those around Israel! There was citrus when I was a young girl, but the freezes in the eighties killed most of the groves. Florida citrus is now grown largely in South Florida, and the growers there are struggling with new diseases and competition from Brazil."

"I do not think I have ever been to Florida. Maybe my father has?" Salem asked as she turned her glance toward Khalil.

"Yes," Khalil responded. "Sara and I went there shortly after we were married. We got married in Sara's parent's Methodist church. My mother and father were not able to afford to come, and we certainly could not afford to bring them nor could Sara's parents. I know my mother was very upset, which put me in a minor depression. Sara thought it would be a good idea to take a vacation to relieve the stress. She had a friend in a small town in Florida—Dunedin—do you know where that is, Martha? Anyway, we both thought a visit to Florida might be fun—kind of a honeymoon."

Martha smiled. "Of course, it is on the west coast near St. Petersburg."

"Well," Khalil continued, "Sara and I thought it would be a nice diversion. We also thought it somewhat ironic that Dunedin is another name for Edinburgh, which is where Sara's roots are on her father's side—red hair and all! Her great-grandfather migrated to America sometime in the late nineteenth century, eventually finding his way west to Illinois."

"Forgive my digression. Anyway, this trip to Florida was a real experience. It turned out that Sara's friend, who actually had been her roommate as an undergraduate, had come to Florida to work as a surgical nurse. Well, she had met this man with whom she was living with when we arrived. He went by a single name—Wiley. I do not think that was his real name, but anyway, he was—how do you say in America—a piece of work. He was part Greek and part Seminole Indian and very striking in appearance. He hardly ever wore shoes or a shirt, and he spent much of his time in or on the water. I think he knew everything there is to know about Florida—the plants, the animals, the history, the hydrology, the geology—everything. He took us places and showed us amazing things. It was, I think, in many ways, the most exhilarating two weeks I have ever experienced. We went to beautiful hidden springs. We snorkeled for scallops and scuba dove for lobsters. We saw manatees and dolphins. We kayaked around lush green mangrove islands and caught fish—wonderful fish like snook and redfish and snapper. We spent evenings on the beach on Honeymoon Island. We visited the Everglades and met some of his Seminole relatives, and we spent a day with his grandmother at the old Greek community in Tarpon Springs, and she cooked the most wonderful Greek dinner. And we always ate outside with a nice bottle of wine and seafood we had caught ourselves. And the conversations were equally exhilarating.

This guy, Wiley, had a free mind that took excursions into politics, religion, and science, and he welcomed debate on any controversy. He looked like a beach bum, but he was one of the most interesting and intelligent persons I have ever met. I have no idea what he did for a living, but he obviously did something, for he seemed to have sufficient money. I remember to this day what he said about God, 'I experienced during my childhood in Florida a communication with what I mentally visualized as a benevolent entity, a critical order and complexity, created by the coordinated interactions of all the physical and biological components that make up Florida's ecology. I discovered God not as a humanlike deity solely concerned with the works and concerns of humans but as a more expansive force, which gave life to the earth and to each life a gift of happiness in offering its contributions to the sustenance of life.'

"Now, when you talk to Nadim, he will tell you this is an overly romantic description of God, but then this guy *was* overly romantic in every sense. Everything he saw, he described in magical terms. He would have driven Nadim crazy—you will see what I mean when you have a chance to talk with Nadim."

"Father, you never told me about this time in Florida," Salem noted.

"Well, I should have because it was when and where you were conceived. I am sure of it!" Khalil continued. "Anyway, one night, Wiley and I started comparing the plight of the Seminoles with the Palestinians. It turns out there are similarities. They both were pushed out of their homes and their cultures threatened by a new intruding culture. And both were forced to become immigrants and refugees. I did not know this, but the Seminoles were largely transported to Oklahoma, just like the Cherokees. A few escaped, however, and found refuge in the Everglades—these are called the Miccosukee—led by a great leader by the name of Abiaca, called Sam Jones by the whites. Wiley was part Miccosukee, and he claims relation to old Abiaca although I am not sure that is the case. Wiley referred to him as the Old Rat Snake. Wiley took me to several Miccosukee villages along Tamiami trail and deeper into the Everglades, and I spent two days providing what medical help I could in spite of the grumbling by the old medicine men. It was that experience that made me think about doing the same for the Palestinian children. No, I don't talk about Wiley much, and I have not heard from him since our visit as he eventually broke up with Sara's friend, but he had a significant influence on my life."

"Well, I can relate somewhat with Wiley," Martha replied. "I spent a great deal of my childhood enjoying Florida's natural beauty. When I was growing up, there were a number of magnificent springs near my home. The water was so clear it looked as though the fish were flying. You could read "In God We Trust" on a coin lying on the bottom in twenty feet of water. I could indeed feel a presence when I was in nature, I just never thought of calling it God. I was taught that God looked like a person and was most concerned about people and that all other animals were there just to serve man. I never thought that was very fair, but we could not question the church."

"Yes, well, perhaps we can explore that later tonight," Khalil said. "Right now, I need to get our luggage upstairs. You get Dahlia as your roommate tonight, Martha."

"Fine with me," Martha replied with a smile. "Let me help with the luggage." She realized that Khalil was not ready to get too involved in a serious conversation. She thought he probably wanted to wait until Nadim was home and Dahlia was in bed.

When Martha and Khalil arrived at the car, Martha commented that her looking so much like Khalil's wife must have been why he came over to talk with her at the café in Bethlehem. He said that was only part of the reason. He said he hesitated at first until he noticed what she was reading. He said he saw no reason to mention her resemblance to Sara. He knew she would find out as soon as Salem saw her. Nadim had noticed also in the parking lot but only whispered his acknowledgment to Khalil.

Martha thought for a while, trying to decide if his nondisclosure was an injurious deception. She felt it was not and decided to forget about it. *As if* she *were an angel!* she thought. She had chosen not to make a complete disclosure to Phil regarding her travelling with Khalil to Haifa. The old adage crossed her mind—What an entangled web we weave when first we practice to deceive.

When they returned upstairs, Martha was hit by the most delicious aroma. "What is that smell!" she asked.

"It is lamb meat with spices I am cooking to put in my *maqloobeh*. That is what we are having for dinner," Salem said.

"Explain maqloobeh," Martha said.

"Well," Salem answered, "it is an upside-down rice and meat dish. Every family has their own recipe. My father's mother—my grandmother—taught me this one. She said it goes back centuries, but I often wondered about that. The secret to our recipe is the baharat—which is a spice mixture. The ingredients are a family secret, but you will be able to identify some of them, like the ginger."

"It smells delicious!" Martha replied as she walked into the kitchen to observe Salem in action.

"Well, we do not have it very often, and it is Nadim's favorite, so he is going to be very grateful for your visiting us!"

CHAPTER 17

After spending about ten minutes in the kitchen, Martha excused herself so she could take a shower and change clothes. When she returned, Nadim had just walked in the door. He had his back to Martha, complaining to Salem and Dahlia about the traffic.

"Hello, Nadim," Martha said, letting him know she was in the room.

Nadim turned and greeted Martha. "Hello, Martha. How was your excursion with Khalil?"

"Great! Speaking of Khalil, where is he?" Martha inquired.

"He went down the street to talk with some old friends. He should be back shortly," Salem answered.

"I guess you know by now how much you look like my mother-in-law?" Nadim said to Martha.

"Oh yes. I think it really shocked Salem. It shocked me also as Khalil had conveniently forgotten to let me know," Martha replied with a sly smile.

"My father is known to practice selective disclosure. It drove my mother crazy sometimes," Salem noted.

"We call this practice sneaky in America. In the South, we sometimes call it little white lies," Martha said with a smile.

"Is nondisclosure the same as a lie?" Nadim wondered.

"You're the professor, you tell us," challenged Salem.

"If it were a purposeful deception with malicious intent, it certainly would qualify as a lie. When used to spare someone's feelings or avoid their embarrassment, perhaps not. Like everything in the world, it depends upon the situation," Nadim commented. "It is like the story of your little white lies and Jimmy Carter who, according to his mother, Lillian, never lied. When a reporter came to his mother's house to conduct an interview, the reporter asked if it were true that her son never told a lie. When Lillian said that was indeed true, the reporter persisted, insisting that no one was perfect and it was not reasonable to state that her son never told a lie. Lillian then conceded that perhaps he had told a few little white lies, to which the reporter responded that a lie was a lie, and that even little white lies counted as lies. Lillian objected, saying that she did not see it that way, and that little white lies served a purpose of protecting cordiality and avoiding rudeness. 'For example,' Lillian said, 'when I invited you in and said it was nice to welcome you to my home—that was a little white lie.'"

Martha laughed when she heard Nadim's story about Ms. Lillian. Growing up, she had known a number of Southern ladies just like her—proper, polite but intelligent, strong, and firm in their convictions and in their protection of family and Southern traditions.

Martha then thought of how quickly Nadim's mind went into an analytical mode, even when contemplating what Martha thought was a rather trivial matter. Martha knew she was in for an interesting evening. She had not engaged in such discourse in a long time and was a bit intimidated. Nonetheless, she looked forward to having an extended conversation after dinner.

When Khalil returned from his visit, he was carrying a couple of bottles of wine.

"Our good neighbors gave us two bottles of Israeli wine—not kosher, however. Have you had Israeli wine before, Martha?" Khalil asked.

Now, Martha was somewhat embarrassed. "Well, no. In fact, I do not drink alcohol."

"Oh yes, I forgot that drinking is not allowed in many of the American churches," Khalil remarked.

"Well. It really has nothing to do with my church. It has to do with the fact that I am a reformed alcoholic. I have not had a drink in over ten years, and if I want to have any type of enjoyable life, I must keep that stretch going," Martha replied, recognizing her disclosure might not be well received.

"How very insensitive of me," Khalil responded. "Does it bother you if people around you drink?"

"Not at all," Martha said.

"OK then, wine for the rest of us, tea for Martha," Khalil remarked as he placed the two bottles on the table.

Martha was puzzled somewhat by how Khalil reacted to her disclosure. Usually, people patronized her with a concerned look and an "I am so sorry" or "How brave of you." Khalil just accepted it without question or without inquiry. It was just the way she wished most people would respond. Martha knew she was dealing with a man of many life experiences. He was both sensitive and emotional, but he applied his sensitivities and emotions wisely. As a doctor, he likely dealt with alcoholism with some frequency and understood the dark side of such addictions. He apparently felt no need to have Martha regurgitate all the painful memories associated with her drinking. It was a story he had heard before.

Nor did he judge her. Quite often, people recoiled when she told them about her alcoholism and then treated her as if she were contaminated or dreadfully diseased. There was no change in expression or body language with Khalil, or with Nadim or Salem for that matter, for they all had heard the conversation.

And so Martha dismissed the issue as irrelevant, which, for her, was quite a relief. However, for reasons well beyond the alcohol issue, Martha could not help but feel she was a damaged person who, through what appeared a strange series of events, found herself in the company of a well-balanced, mentally healthy, intelligent, and thoughtful family. It was a feeling she had experienced before in her life, and she began to sense those impulses of inferiority slip into her thought stream. This time, however, she rejected them. *These people like me,* she thought. *They do not want to judge me, so I am going to just be myself. They will need to decide whether they can accept who I am. I am not going to try to mold myself into what I think they want me to be! That is a habit I am bringing to an end!*

—✦—

CHAPTER 18

—✦—

A chime sounded in the kitchen, and Salem rushed to retrieve her dinner from the oven. Nadim, who had been standing, slowly moved over to the sofa and collapsed with a sigh. "A challenging day—first week of classes," he said as he stretched his arms. "Khalil, how about opening one of those bottles?"

"Sure," Khalil said as he moved into the kitchen to find a corkscrew and a couple of glasses. "Do you want some, Noor?"

Salem, who was in the middle of flipping her maqloobeh, glanced quickly at her father, shaking her head. "Not now—later. Thanks."

While Khalil was opening the wine, Dahlia came running into the room and jumped onto her father's lap. "I love you, Daddy!" she exclaimed.

"Well, not only are you speaking English now, you are speaking American. Did Martha teach you that?" Nadim asked.

Dahlia giggled with excitement. "Yes, Daddy," She obviously had never heard the word *daddy* before and was delighted with this new discovery.

"What does she usually call you, Nadim?" Martha asked.

"Baba, which is kind of a Lebanese slant on the Arabic *Abbi*. Older kids today often use Dad or Daddy, but we had not taught this to Dahlia yet—only Momma. I guess it is my new name," Nadim said with a grin.

Dahlia then ran to Martha, giving her a big hug. "I love you too, Martha," she squealed.

This caught Martha by surprise, and she found herself tearing up. Such exuberance and happiness—it was so refreshing. She found herself wondering what it would have been like to have had a daughter.

"'Youth is wasted on the young,' so said Mark Twain. But I don't think Dahlia wastes anything," Khalil commented as Dahlia rushed out of the room to her bedroom, singing as she went. "She is a joy in a world in need of joy. But then, to be honest, so was her mother, at least, until the hormones kicked in. I remember when she brought this skinny, curly haired scarecrow to our house. My first thought was that she had picked up some vagrant off the street so we could feed him. Now she is married to him. She could have married a rich doctor—I knew plenty of them. And she was—and still is—a real beauty. They would have fallen all over themselves to marry Salem. But no, she picks a destitute intellect—an absentminded professor."

Of course, Khalil was looking at Nadim as he said this and was smiling the whole time. It was obvious he and Nadim had a special connection—far beyond being in-laws.

And Nadim would have been remiss if he did not counter Khalil's pseudo-insult. "Well, I was really impressed when I met Salem's mother, but then she introduced me to Khalil. The first word that entered my head was *megalomaniac*, the second was *recalcitrant*. This man had a mind that had been closed for decades, and try as I would, I could not open it. He remains, to this day, the most stubborn human being I have ever met. If Salem were not so enchanting and so beautiful, I would have sprinted to the front door."

"They do this all the time, Martha. Just ignore it. They adore each other—and they are both very stubborn," Salem said, laughing.

"I think I understand. In America, we also often use insult as a form of expressing affection. Can I help you in the kitchen, Salem?" Martha replied as she rose from her chair.

"Sure," Salem said. "Get five plates from the cabinet. We will serve the plates here in the kitchen, that way we do not clutter up the dining room table."

CHAPTER 19

Martha had never thought of cooking as an art form. Rather, cooking was a tradition that required patience, skill, and knowledge but not any particularly high level of creativity, nor did it invite a great deal of experimentation. Southern food is wonderful in a comforting sort of way. Cornbread, black-eyed peas, collard greens, okra and tomatoes, peach cobbler, grits and eggs, fried chicken, chicken and rice, ham hocks and lima beans—she loved all these. She found the Midwest food was somewhat less imaginative—beef and potatoes, rhubarb pie, white beans and shredded beef on toast. It is what Phil liked, but Martha missed her Southern meals and would often try to get Phil to adjust. Once, she fixed grits and eggs with hickory smoked sausage for breakfast. But he had a fit and wouldn't touch it. It was back to fried eggs, bacon, and hash browns.

And while Southern cuisine called for a more diverse use of spices than Midwestern food, it could not compare to Salem's maqloobeh (except for Louisiana Cajun, of course). The spices sang to her long before she put anything into her mouth. And when she did finally get to the tasting phase of the meal, she was totally astonished. It was the most wonderful thing she had ever tasted, and she let Salem know this.

"This is wonderful—I think the best food I have ever tasted. Salem, you are a culinary artist!" Martha exclaimed.

Of course, there is no higher compliment than to express true joy with someone's cooking. Salem beamed when Martha offered this testimony. "Thank you! I did not hear anyone else's opinion?" Salem said, looking at the two men at the table.

"We are too busy stuffing our mouths to express our appreciation," Nadim said slyly. "It is wonderful, as always. I guess we do take it for granted although we do not get maqloobeh every day, especially with lamb. She normally makes it with chicken."

"Well, we have a special guest today," Salem answered.

"And we are not special?" Khalil responded.

"You know what I mean. Family is also special but in a different way," Salem said, laughing.

Martha watched the interaction of the three of them and wondered if families could really be this close and this loving. Did they ever fight or lie to each other? Did they ever get on one another 's nerves? It almost seemed too perfect.

"You know, Salem, I am not sure your father told me if you had a career. Do you work outside of being a mother and wife? Which I know all too well is a demanding and often thankless job in itself," Martha inquired.

"Like my mother, I am a nurse. I work three days a week at a local hospital—well, you would probably call it a clinic," Salem said.

"Who takes care of Dahlia when you work?" Martha asked, looking over at Dahlia, who was now sitting at the table.

"Nadim's sister if Nadim is not home. She lives three houses down with her husband and two young children—a boy and a girl. Dahlia is very close to her cousins. Of course, Dahlia has just started her schooling. So during the daytime, she is often in class," Salem said.

"Where does Dahlia go to school?" Martha asked.

"Right now, we have her in a private school," Nadim noted.

"Are not there adequate public schools?" Martha asked

"There are, but there are some issues that we can discuss later," Nadim said as he nodded toward Dahlia. Obviously, this was a delicate matter that he did not want to discuss with Dahlia present.

"I understand. Later," Martha acknowledged.

After everyone had finished eating, Salem put her hand on Dahlia's shoulder and said, "Dahlia, it is time to get ready for bed. You have to get up early tomorrow for school. Tell everyone good night."

Dahlia, sobbing silently, went around the table and gave each person a long hug, including Martha. When she got to Martha, she said, "Do not forget you are sleeping in my room tonight."

"I won't, honey. I will see you in the morning," Martha said.

Dahlia, who had stopped crying, now began laughing. "She called me honey. What does that mean?"

Nadim explained in Arabic, which made Dahlia smile. "You are a honey also!" she said as she hugged Martha's neck. And then she went skipping with her mother into her bedroom.

CHAPTER 20

When Salem returned, she collected the plates and disappeared into the kitchen. Martha offered to help, but Salem insisted she remain seated. Shortly, she returned with four coffee cups and a plate of what Martha thought were small cookies covered in sesame seeds.

"We like Turkish-style coffee with a little green cardamom added," Salem commented. "I hope you like it. If you want, you can add some honey. These desserts are called *barazek*. I would like to take credit for them, but my sister-in-law made them. They are quite delicious."

Martha lifted the cup of coffee and took a sip. She nodded an approval as she took a bite of the barazek. She smiled and said, "Wonderful, so nutty, yet sweet. Thank you."

As they all three enjoyed the coffee and dessert, Martha could tell that Nadim was ready to talk.

"Martha, you lived in the South during much of the civil rights activism, I assume?" Nadim began. "Therefore, you know full well the damage that can be caused by discrimination and segregation. While there are differences between the plight of the African Americans during those years and the Palestinians in Israel, the West Bank and Gaza today, there are also many similarities. You may know that Arab Israeli children do not go to the same public schools as Jewish children. The government can give a thousand reasons why they think this is necessary, but it is not really any different than what they called separate but equal in the South. There is indeed separation, but there is a paucity of equality. Palestinians are second-class citizens in Israel. Our family is lucky for we have enough money and education to protect us from much of the pain felt by the average Arab in Israel. For many, there is no escape from poverty because they cannot secure equal opportunity.

"However, there are those in Israel, including a substantial number of Jews, who think the system needs to be reformed. I work with such groups who are trying to promote joint Arab-Hebrew schools. On a comparatively small scale, it has been tested, but more needs to be done to make it fully successful. There is a joint school about twenty miles south of the University of Haifa, but commuting would be very difficult for us although not impossible. Right now, Dahlia is in kindergarten at a private Christian Orthodox school that is quite good, and both Christians and Muslims go there. But I want Dahlia to escape the segregation. In my opinion, just as in your country, if Israeli society does not integrate Arab and Hebrew societies, it will decay from inside. I think I can safely say that more than just a few Jewish citizens feel this way as well."

Nadim stopped for a while, cleaned his glasses, and then continued. "But this issue is but a symptom of a much larger dilemma. And understanding this dilemma and exploring and developing ways for resolution is what I do for a living, not only by teaching international relations and social justice, but by writing and communicating some of the social theories we—my colleagues and I—have introduced over the years. We have drawn these theories from extensive study of works conducted by other researchers in a number of disciplines, as well as from our own experimentation and observation.

"And I can summarize the nature of this dilemma with a rather straightforward question. What critical changes in human social behavior and social structure are needed to ensure long-term survival of the global human community, and how do we facilitate such changes? I clearly believe that our present patterns of behavior are not going to accommodate this directive for long-term survival. If we continue to insist upon embracing divisions among us built upon prejudices and fail to fully grasp our relationship with the super-organism we call earth, we will hasten the demise of our cultures and our societies.

"When I was twelve, my father and mother were killed in Lebanon during the civil war. I was devastated, for I loved my parents deeply. My father was a great man, a man of peace, a man of far-reaching intelligence. He was not a man of the church, but he was a man of Jesus. My mother was his equal in these respects, a person so loving that she earned the awe and respect of the entire community. Neither was bashful in offering criticism to those who used hatred and violence to gain power or to impose an ideology. This is why they were killed, I believe.

"My first reaction, of course, was to seek revenge. But revenge against whom—the Maronite Philangists? The PLO? The Israelis? The CIA? Hezbollah? Syria? They all could have been behind these murders.

"My next emotional reaction was to blame religion—all religion. It was religion that created this situation that led to the civil war, I thought. But as I thought further, I realized it was not religion, it was people. It was people who used religion to justify their xenophobia, their prejudices, their hatred, their use of violence. Religion was just a handy conduit for threatened and angry people to express their hatred. If religion were not available, these people would have found some other convenient excuse to behave badly. In fact, I asked myself, is it possible that religion might actually contribute to better behavior in people? At first, this seemed inconsistent with my observations, but then I thought about examples in which religion was rejected—such as Stalinist Russia, which was an atheist state. They managed to find excuses for wholesale slaughter without religious justification. Perhaps, in spite of its vulnerability to abuses, religion actually attenuated hatefulness within a society. No, I concluded, I could not blame religion. The cause of such behavior had to find genesis in something more innate, something ingrained within the survival directive within our genetic coding.

"And then in 1987, just as I was getting ready to enter university, two experiences helped bring certain features of human behavior into focus—I read Richard Dawkins's *The Selfish Gene,* and I saw the movie *The Mission.*

"Dawkins revealed two concepts that brought a biological perspective into my consideration of why there is religion and why there is such division among groups. The first concept revolves around assignment of the gene itself as the basic unit of evolution, or what is known as gene-centered evolution—hence the term *selfish gene.* The second is that human social evolution is influenced by cultural evolution, which relies upon the storage and generational transfer of learned information and developed technology through what Dawkins called 'memes.' Upon reading Dawkins's book, I began to formulate a social evolutionary theory called the anthropocentric strategy, which I will explain shortly.

"The movie, *The Mission,* made me aware of the importance of religion in both promoting altruism and cooperation on the one hand and its vulnerability to political abuses that can distort and diminish its beneficent foundation on the other hand. In the case of this movie, the religion was Christianity—Catholicism, specifically. But the same issues likely have arisen with most other religions. I guess the question that came to my mind was—why do we even have religion?"

Nadim paused for a while then turned to Martha. "I know from talking to Khalil that you are a member of a rather fundamentalist

Protestant church, so I am going to ask you to consider what I am about to present with objectivity. Remember, I embrace the basic tenants of love, respect, and peace upon which the Abrahamic religions are founded—these being Judaism, Christianity, and Islam. I also recognize that there are contradictions within the Bible and the Qur'an regarding the use of violence against others, and that I cannot fully reconcile these inconsistencies."

Martha, looking directly into Nadim's eyes, acknowledged her desire to remain objective. Nadim then continued.

"If we are ever going to truly understand ourselves—and such understanding is a critical first step in resolving our dilemma—we must accept the biological reality that human beings are indeed animals and that there is strong fossil and genetic evidence that we are primate mammals who evolved and developed in Africa. About one hundred thousand years ago, human groups began to move northward from Africa, presumably to follow the animal herds. These humans migrated into the Levant and Europe and, after some time, into Asia and the Western hemisphere. At this time, the climate was influenced by an interglacial period, meaning the ice sheets were retreating northward, which opened up regions to more temperate ecological systems more amenable to human sustenance.

"So as hunters and gatherers, these migrating humans established a critical dependence upon the ecological stability of their expansive territory. It would make sense then that any belief system they adopted would be oriented around this dependence. We certainly see this, for example, in the cave paintings of Europe. These people would visualize themselves as participants in the complex ecosystem that surrounded them, and accordingly, they would understand, in very real terms, the need for successful reproduction of their prey species; the impact of weather, season, and climate; and the importance of the physical layout of the landscape. We would call their belief system animistic paganism in today's terms, meaning, they believed nature was organized and operated by some type of omnipresent force or spirit. Dawkins would likely call this force the laws of science. Buckminster Fuller referred to it as synergy, and Jane Goodall, another famous British zoologist, talks of it in more spiritual terms—although the term *spiritual* is certainly imbued with a certain degree of ambiguity. Our early ancestors often envisioned this directing force as the combined efforts of one or more spiritual entities."

Khalil interrupted, "This philosophy of an organizing force or spirit applied to all life systems is what I was talking about earlier, Martha, when I was discussing my friend Wiley." Khalil then related to Nadim Wiley's quote regarding God.

Nadim rolled his eyes slightly, then commented, "Well, that puts a romantic slant on the concept, and it is perhaps similar to the feelings Jane Goodall has expressed in her writings. But the more hardcore evolutionary biologists like Dawkins and Harvard's E. O. Wilson typically avoid such romantic embellishments. They tend to see only the laws of chemistry and physics as the directing forces, with no evidence of any noble, far-reaching purpose that would imply a purposeful creation. Of course, this is where science and religion can often butt heads—as we might discuss later.

"This human population some hundred thousand years ago, then, is the backdrop for considering the influence of this selfish gene. If Dawkins is correct, the collection of genes within a human individual of that time was able to survive because they were quite successful in replicating themselves, meaning, they were beneficiaries of natural selection. Remember, at any time in the biological history of the earth, the gene collection of all life represents survivors, and they are survivors because they facilitated a strategy that allowed them to replicate in spite of the stresses imposed by the environment. Of course, as stresses changed, the gene collection adjusted—thus there was always a changing set of survivors. The rate of this change we usually think of as being directly related to the amplitude and frequency of fluctuations within the environment.

"Adaptations that allow long-term survival include manipulation of the behavior of the carrying organism by the controlling gene collection—or as Dawkins would say, the organism was merely the gene-carrying vehicle. These impacted behaviors include such things as the mating urge, territorial protection, countering competition for mating rights, mate selection, and in more complex animals such as humans, a sense of altruism directed toward those who share genes—hence, the term, *kin selection*. The picture that is painted is rather devoid of true compassion, with animals influenced by kin selection actually taking actions that are deleterious to themselves but are overall advantageous to the promotion of their genes by helping or sacrificing for their kin—and the closer the kin, the more likely the individual is to sacrifice its own interest. Think about how true that is—I would give my life without thinking for Dahlia, and I would certainly put myself at risk for a child in the neighborhood but might be much more reluctant for a child in some distant country. And Dawkins even suggests this applies to our relationship with other species—for example, we typically are much more likely to extend help to a dog or a chimpanzee, or even a horse or a lamb, than we would to a toad or a grasshopper. And the reason why we would is because we share a larger percentage of genes with mammals than amphibians or insects. It all really depends upon a mathematical review. Is there a greater benefit as measured by the magnitude of gene replication than there is detriment as measured by gene loss associated with personal sacrifice? Put in these terms, the concepts of compassion, altruism, and love are condensed down to issues of statistics and gene replication. This is a bit insulting, I suppose, for it is suggestive that when I lay my life down for Dahlia, it is not because I care so much for her as an individual, it is because she is an extension of my genetic identity and, hence, capable of sustaining my selfish genes. My caring is only an impulse sent through my genes as a convenient behavioral adaptation."

At this point, Martha interrupted. "Nadim, that seems cold. Certainly you do not think your love for Dahlia finds genesis solely from some subconscious statistical analysis that determines her protection is a good investment genetically?"

"Well, no, I do not feel that. But I must be objective. Perhaps love is a behavioral adaptation that emerged through natural selection. That does not make it any less authentic. But let's save a more detailed discussion of love for later," Nadim replied. He then stood up to stretch and went to the kitchen to pour himself some more coffee. When he returned, he continued his explanation.

—ᴡᴏᴄᴄᴛᴏᴄᴛᴏᴏᴏᴡ—

CHAPTER 21

—ᴡᴏᴄᴄᴛᴏᴄᴛᴏᴏᴏᴡ—

"**S**o we can now envision this group of hunter-gatherer humans closely aligned with the ecological dynamics of their territory. They fully recognize they are a part of this dynamic. Their life is about survival within the range of diurnal and seasonal fluctuations within their environment. And because they are able to transfer helpful information about the state of their understanding and their technology through memes, the group grows more efficient by improving on tools and techniques with each generation, and memes can often facilitate adaptations much faster than genes. This often helps bring stability and ecological success.

"Things then were going along quite well for these migrant humans until about twenty-thousand years ago when the climate began to change. Their selfish genes were directing their behavior such that the efficiency of gene replication was high—and these genes were interwoven within not only the human population but within the population of other species. And the belief system reflected this behavioral direction. An animistic view of the world ensured the balance was attended to, and energies were directed in a manner that accommodated the mathematical game of outpacing detriments with benefits.

"And then the climate and, accordingly, the environment began changing. A new glacial period was setting in, and the ice sheets were extending southward. This posed new challenges for this successful and aware hunter-gatherer human group. What they had learned regarding new tools and hunting weapons and the migration patterns of the herds and ambush methods and the seasonal patterns of small animals and the plant communities were growing less relevant. Their Neanderthal neighbors had already disappeared, impacted by the changing ecology and competition from *Homo sapiens*. Now the sapiens community was under assault, and they had to find an effective way to adapt. And here the selfish gene faced a dilemma and a new set of conditions from which to conduct the statistical evaluation related to the balance of detriments to benefits.

"Remember that the behavioral patterns established through the controlling selfish genes were oriented around preservation of those with whom the vehicle organism shared genes. Also the vigor with which one protected those who shared these genes was directly proportional to the percentage of genes shared. In addition, this pattern was ingrained within an animistic belief system, which one would think would make change more difficult to accept. It would not be unlike telling a Christian or a Muslim to give up their dogma—a dogma that was ingrained into their culture. I would suspect then that, starting about twenty thousand years ago, times grew ever more tumultuous for our ancient relatives. Change or perish!"

Martha then interrupted Nadim. "If these genes directed the individual to show compassion and altruism toward those with whom they shared common genes, then why has there been so much war among various tribes who obviously were very closely related genetically?"

Nadim looked at her with a serious look, then answered, "From a male perspective, it is about egg protection. From a female perspective, it is about mate selection. Remember, a male must fertilize the egg with his sperm to gain the maximum benefit of gene replication. The female is assured maximum gene replication regardless of who her mate is, but she does need to be selective in picking a mate in an effort to maximize survival of her offspring.

"So a male may share genes with another male within another tribe or even his own tribe, but there is no benefit to sharing the eggs held by the females he controls with this other male as this greatly reduces the percentage of his genes being replicated. Hence, the detriment to giving up your egg reserves is greater than the benefits from tolerating a competing male, even if he is kin. Remember, from an evolutionary perspective, it is about statistics. Hence, the competition for eggs is intense among males. This should be no surprise to you as we see clear examples of this among many animals, including humans."

Nadim then continued his discourse. "Now, let's get back to this struggling group of humans. To this point, everything I have related to you on development of human society has been discussed ad infinitum within the scientific community and will continue to be reviewed as new data become available. There certainly are variations on this theme, but in general, what I have offered represents a logical hypothesis based upon existing information.

"But now, let's get more theoretical and controversial. These intelligent, culturally sophisticated human beings were facing extermination as their environment changed beyond their social, cultural, and biological abilities to survive under the status quo operational strategy. Quite obviously, this strategy needed to change. This is easily said but more difficult to actually implement. I give, as an example, Easter Island as discussed by the famous American biologist Jared Diamond in his book *Collapse*. In summary, the population of this island continued their practice of deforestation to subsidize their religious practices even when it was obvious that their culture was self-destructing. Think about the global community today—aren't we facing similar situations?

"Therefore, while some people might argue that these people—these hunter-gatherers twenty-thousand years ago—with their ability of rational thought, over a period of time, would choose to abandon their belief systems and would develop a new belief system that was more attentive to their needs, I would argue that changing belief systems, even in the face of extinction, was not always the option selected. Any new belief system would require that they envision humans as segregated from the complex dynamics of nature, as these dynamics were becoming more restrictive regarding access to the available resources. Remember, they envisioned all components of their environment as sacred and spiritual, and preserving this environment was integral to their survival. Now this environment was trying to kill them—it was abandoning them, so they needed to abandon it and take from nature rather than just waiting patiently to receive from nature.

"From a cultural perspective, old ways die hard, but it is possible, I suppose, that over time, after facing catastrophic conditions, the necessary changes could have happened just through conscious choice. But remember, this belief system was based upon the biological impulse of extending altruism to those with whom you share genes—an impulse that could be called instinctual. So it was not within the behavioral directive as wired by the individual's collection of genes to view nature as the enemy as something that needed to be confronted and subdued. But this was exactly the change that was needed—a dilemma, needless to say.

"Now, suppose there was a behavior directing gene which was present in many forms—what we call alleles—and that most of these forms directed the organism to respond to kin selection by extending altruism to others, human and nonhuman, proportional to the extent of common genetic heritage. This would have been the dominant pattern within our human group some twenty thousand years ago. But imagine one allele, when partnered with an identical allele—what we call homozygous—solicits a different behavior.

Instead of directing the individual to proportionally attend to the needs of all shared genes, it accommodates only those genes unique to the human species. This then would allow the introduction of a new strategy—the anthropocentric strategy, where only humans are important and all other aspects of the environment, living and nonliving, are made available for full-scale exploitation without consideration of impacts upon our nonhuman shared-gene partners. Do you follow this?"

Martha hesitated a while and then responded, "It appears somewhat analogous to the situation we see with cancer. When a malignant cell escapes the control of the organizational directives of the body, it is free to spread in any direction and consume resources at a pace that maximizes its proliferation in spite of the fact that it will eventually destroy itself by killing the source of these resources—greed and selfishness in its most lethal form."

Nadim nodded in agreement. "Yes. While I think we have to be careful in using this example, for I am not sure the parallels are consistent, it does nonetheless offer verification that such self-destructive selfish patterns and strategies can occur. It is very possible, biologically, that such behavioral influencing alleles could exist.

"Now, consider this new strategy emerging within, say, a few individuals at that time. Prior to the changing environment, this allele would likely not been successful in expressing itself. It was imbedded but latent within the population, and it survived because it demonstrated its characteristics only in the homozygous state. But with the population some twenty thousand years ago dwindling because of the changing climate, it is not difficult to imagine a few of these homozygous individuals joining forces to burn down large tracts of land, to kill off competing predators on a wholesale basis without their conscience paying a price, to capture herd animals and manipulating them into domestication, to dam rivers and drain wetlands, and generally, impose their will upon the environment as needed to ensure their survival.

"Their success then would take on cultural significance. A new belief system emerged to replace the old animistic system. Eventually, this new belief system became monotheistic with a single omnipotent God emerging, who favored humans and gave them permission to change their environment as they saw necessary to survive. The worship of idols and images of the old spirits and gods was abandoned and prohibited. There is but one God, and that God made man in his image and provided the environment for the sole use of man. This is a very convenient support system for this new anthropocentric strategy. So genetic shifts, combined with cultural adaptations and the high developmental advantage offered by memes, facilitated the development of civilization. And this involved not just agriculture but the segregation of the human species from their genetic partners manifested as other species. In fact, humans coming to become insulted by the suggestion that they were animals, with the term *animal* coming to mean something that was base, brutal, and malevolent. And so over the past thirteen thousand years, plus or minus, the anthropocentric strategy has come to dominate most cultures and has allowed those cultures to impose themselves on any who operate under the old animistic strategy. For example, look at the encounter between the Europeans and the Native Americans some five hundred plus years ago. We know who won out in that situation. I believe the same type of encounter occurred much earlier in the Levant.

"But I do not believe that is all there is to the story. It is my opinion and the opinion of others that the anthropocentric strategy now needs to change in a way that permits us to establish sustainable practices in our dealings with the earth, for sustainability relates to survival. Like the cancer cells you referenced, we cannot continue to expend resources at a rate faster than their replenishment, for once expended, they are gone, and yet our reliance upon them will remain. This strategy cannot sustain our existing system—that is scientifically and mathematically demonstrable. This need for sustainability then requires a new belief system. And while I believe scientific understanding is a critical element to this new belief system, I personally sense that more is required than just reliance upon science. And this is where religion becomes important. And to discuss the role of religion, we must enter the realm of abstractions."

CHAPTER 22

Nadim pushed himself up from the chair and stretched. He suggested they take a brief rest before he continued. Martha excused herself to go to the restroom. When she returned, she saw Nadim and Khalil standing in the kitchen, having a quiet conversation. They returned to the living room after about five minutes.

Khalil turned briefly to Martha. "Nadim is going to get into what he would call an objective review of religion that I hope you do not find offensive. He may say some things that a born-again Christian may not appreciate. If it gets too unbearable, let him know."

Martha sighed softly. "I am not easily offended. I now realize I came to Israel to think about my faith and the foundation of my beliefs. I can make up my own mind and am not threatened by other peoples' opinions. Please continue."

Nadim sat back into his chair and then proceeded with his comments. "While many people think of the beliefs of any one religion as being staid, recalcitrant dogma that are not to be questioned or changed, history tells a different story. If we read the Old Testament, and even parts of the New Testament and the Qur'an, we can find some very brutal, even barbaric, practices when compared to today's religious teachings and social laws. Except in the rare case of the most extreme sects and governments—which we often call terrorists—our present civilization and its religious institutions do not think of stoning people to death for adultery or committing genocide to serve God's will and directive. Any government that does condone such things is considered backward and is openly criticized and challenged by almost all religious and political leaders.

"So it is reasonable to say then, that religion, like all dynamic things, undergoes evolution. What changes typically are passages and references that were included to accommodate the cultural norms or political realities at the time of the writing. And of course, these various passages and references are reviewed and discarded at different rates. Most are eventually abandoned, and if some are retained, they often become imbedded within a tradition or symbolic rituals. Unfortunately, there is a tendency by some to take these words literally, and this can create frustration and confusion. In the worst cases, this literal interpretation can solicit violence and chaos. Such instances often are promoted by persons who claim to be direct agents of God. This is the evil to which religion is most vulnerable.

"But I want to focus on what I call the beneficent foundation of religion. The call for love, peace, respect, patience, and forgiveness permeates the Abrahamic religions and most other recognized religions for that matter. Jesus, in particular, was clearly a pacifist and believed in the power of tolerance and love.

"I do believe there are very tangible reasons Jesus emphasized these things. I find it interesting that while some people may envision compassion and pacifism as a weakness, these attributes can, in reality, stabilize society—and by stabilize, I also mean increase survival potential. Using the mathematics of what we call game theory, we can illustrate that being sensitive to the needs of others can result in cooperation and a general stabilization of the community. This cooperation may be called altruism or love. Did Jesus and other leaders—religious or otherwise—emphasize love and peace because they knew that a society that adopted them as the base of their operational strategy would be the most stable, the most successful?

"When we watch movies such as *The Mission*, we see both sides of religion. We see the side entangled in politics, involved in power struggles and social manipulation, and then we see the true expression of the message of love and peace. In this story, a young Jesuit priest named Father Gabriel conveys through deeds the teachings of Jesus as he helps local native tribes in Brazil establish social stability and a happy community. At no time during the movie does he talk about saving souls or eternal life. He just purveys love and cooperation. In the end, his own church abandons his efforts, and he is left to martyr himself as the Portuguese slavers crush the mission that he was so instrumental in building. When his and the mission's fate becomes clear, Gabriel questions his faith as he talks for a final time to Brother Rodrigo—an ex-slave trader and mercenary whom Gabriel converted. One is reminded of Jesus at Gethsemane.

'If might is right, and love has no place in the world—I don't have the strength to live in a world like that, Rodrigo.'

"The movie ends with Gabriel's death and the death of all the Jesuits and most of the tribe. It is sad and depressing, and it leaves the impression that Gabriel's efforts were in vain. But in fact, they were not, for the world has since indeed found a place for love. The world Father Gabriel lived in during the eighteenth century condoned slavery, genocide, torture, and classism, as well as persecution based upon gender, race, and religion. There was no unified world effort to bring peace as we have today. While in our time love still is countered by ample amounts of hatred and bigotry and abuse, it receives much more attention than it did in those earlier times, and its importance and influence has grown and, I believe, continues to grow. And we must believe that this persistence of love is due largely to the efforts and persistence of people like Father Gabriel.

"But do these expressions of love and peace represent anything more than a statistical decision to improve one's position and to increase the chances of gene replication, or are there other influences involved? Is there an omnipresent guiding force that promotes love and altruism? Is there God?

"So we must ask, is religion and the acceptance of God—however God may be defined—necessary in the promotion of peace and love, or are they really impediments? Richard Dawkins, in his book *The God Delusion* is quite critical of organized religion and the concept of a personal anthropocentric God. He suggests that the premise that people should accept all the mythology religion offers on faith alone is not reasonable. Dawkins believes that such acceptance opens the system up for abuses—which certainly has been the case over history. On the other hand, if I recall correctly, he does not have solid evidence that the absence of religion would improve the state of the world."

CHAPTER 23

"Perhaps the most troubling facet of most religions is the promise of eternal life as a reward for obedience. This changes the nature of social negotiations if this is believed by the followers, for it devalues our present existence and offers additional reason for self-sacrifice beyond the kin relationship we discussed earlier. A population that firmly believes in an eternal life is much easier to persuade and manipulate. Dawkins finds this most loathsome, and I tend to agree with him.

"First of all, what does eternal life mean? Does it mean eternal consciousness and awareness, or does it simply mean that your acts, if they are remembered as contributing to the welfare or happiness of others, generate a surviving legacy. Is Beethoven eternal, or Gandhi? And of course, we might think of ourselves as eternal because the physical components of our bodies are redistributed to the earth's life cycle after we die. And what about gene replication? If I die, will I continue to live through Dahlia and her children? In a way, that sounds reasonable. But does eternal life mean that you are eternally conscious as implied by many religions? Is there some entity we call a soul that behaves beyond the control of your brain's synapses and, in some manner, allows you to consciously exist forever? And what is forever? Ever since science revealed that time is not constant, can we really conceive of forever? Forever, considered within one context, may be a minute within another.

"And say you were granted an eternal conscious life. What would you do, where would you be? Would you have a young body and enjoy the pleasures of the senses? Would you live in an idyllic paradise? Even such wonderful conditions might get boring after a while. Or is this eternal life enjoyed without the encumbrance of a body, allowing you to drift around the universe as an omnipresent, omniscient force, joyfully watching the daily activities of your living relatives and, in some manner, providing them subtle guidance as they struggle to survive.

"Of course, from a scientific perspective, all this seems unlikely. However, recognizing how bizarre reality actually is now that we know about quantum mechanics and dark energy in space and envision the actual nature of matter on the smallest level through concepts such as string theory and gaze billions of years into the past with our powerful telescopes and contemplate the behavior of black holes, we cannot totally rule out the possible existence of what we call a soul, a perpetual individual consciousness.

"But was eternal life really what Jesus and our other loving pacifist founders of religion and civil society most concerned about? Perhaps someone else conveniently added these references into the religious writings in an effort to win converts? Perhaps we need to reconsider what Jesus and these others were trying to tell us? Martha, how many of your fellow born-again Christians would have embraced the church if eternal life had not been part of the bargain?"

Martha pondered this question for a moment before replying. "Well, it is something our preacher talks about a great deal—a great deal more than he talks about love and peace for sure. I would say most of our congregation places the promise of eternal life as very influential to their decision to accept Jesus as their Savior. Quite honestly, however, it was not a major issue with me. I was lost, I felt unloved, and I was confused about what life really meant. By embracing the offerings of our church, I gained a feeling of belonging, of being loved. Much of that, I suppose, was because of the sense of community—the fact that I was surrounded by people just as lost as I was. But you are right, eternal life is appealing, and after hearing it enough times, you become convinced it is true. It is interesting, though, to hear you analyze the concept in such detail. Our preacher never did that. We all just assumed that eternal life meant going to a place called heaven where you immersed yourself in God's love—and it was never really made clear what that meant. If it is a purposeful deception, it is quite effective. If it is indeed true, then I cannot imagine what is really involved."

Nadim looked Martha directly into her eyes. "You have a very logical and analytical mind, Martha. I am really surprised you embraced the born-again mantra so readily. But then maybe I should not be so quick to criticize. I am sure that your church, in many ways, has helped a great number of people. My concern is that, in my opinion, deception is involved. But then deception is everywhere. The whole anthropocentric strategy is actually a deception."

Martha replied, "Maybe imbedded within these deceptions are some truths, some parcels of wisdom that have allowed us to survive."

"Yes, I think that is true," Salem interjected. She had been so quiet all this time that Martha had thought perhaps she had not been following the discussion. Salem continued. "Let me relate an analogy that I believe summarizes our present perspective of religion—and don't laugh because it is a little, uh, what would you say, silly. Do you remember the movie *The Wizard of Oz*? Well, I see the big green-headed wizard as a metaphor for religion's perception of an anthropocentric god. He was blustery, self-absorbed, and insensitive even though he was touted to be all wise and beneficent. But this green-headed wizard was just a front, a deception. When the real wizard was revealed, he was peaceful, non-imposing, wise, and compassionate—just the opposite of the pseudo-wizard. It is like our religions—they are often implemented as rigid, unforgiving dogma, and yet the basic foundations are respect, humility, love, peace, tolerance, and forgiveness. How such opposing scenarios could emerge from the same set of teachings and documents, I guess, depends upon the interpretation. For example, does 'God's chosen people' mean Israeli Jews have been given divine authority to destroy people's homes with bulldozers, or does it mean they are imbued with a responsibility to help guide all people to a higher level of self-realization through love and compassion? Does jihad mean that Islam has a right to wage violent war against nonbelievers, or does it mean that each individual needs to face his internal struggles to reach a higher level of understanding, love, and humility?

"I would suggest that the operative word here is *love*—as noted in Corinthians, '*Of these the greatest is love.*' And by love, I do not feel its expression is limited to just your particular group or people of your religious beliefs, it must be extended to all life systems, it must be an expression of the sanctity of life."

"Very well put! This is why I married you." Nadim laughed.

"You married me because no one else would have you!" Salem answered, also laughing.

"Well, that may be so, but keeping your metaphor in mind, let's think about where we are in this discussion," Nadim said, still smiling but obviously anxious to escape from his wife's playful attack. "Perhaps I need to wrap up this conversation with a summarization. First of all, we recognize our so-called civilized world—that being a world exclusive of the few remaining vestiges of hunter-gatherer society—abides by what may be called the anthropocentric strategy. We also can see rather clearly that rapid consumption of the earth's resources promoted by this strategy is self-destructive. Therefore, we need to evolve toward a strategy that establishes resource preservation and replenishment at a rate higher than or, at least, equal to our rate of consumption—this being called a sustainable dynamic or, as some scientists would say, a quasi-steady state. Long-term survival is likely only if this is achieved.

"We can end our reliance and promotion of the anthropocentric strategy in two ways—through natural selection or through memes. If we rely upon natural selection, the pathway will likely be very brutal and devastating, for catastrophic conditions will be needed to impose the stresses required to favor the old alleles—those that recognize an animist world, the predominant alleles of over twenty thousand years ago, which we discussed earlier. However, if we rely upon memes, we can use our gained knowledge and our ability for rational thought to change voluntarily, without the need for the catastrophe I mentioned.

"To do this—to rely upon our memes—is going to require extraordinary effort and cooperation from religious leaders, political leaders, and economists, scientists, and engineers, as well as the population at large. It also means facing and successfully challenging those who oppose such adjustments. And there needs to be notable adjustments made. Let me relate just a few of these.

"A new religious covenant needs to be developed in which the beneficent foundation of all the existing religions are used to build upon a love and peace based religion in which economic advantage, violence, and war as a means of gaining advantage or power are rejected and where compassion is used as the basis of all negotiations. This will mean tolerance for other ways of thought and restraint in judging others and restraint in using force on those who do not accept your concept of God. This will mean recognition that this concept of God is a personal matter and that the only requirement for the stability of society is that the foundation of this concept be based upon love, peace, and tolerance. I would imagine this new covenant would include embracing the more animistic perspective of God, one similar to that described by Khalil's friend, Wiley."

"The new covenant could be called neo-pantheism and would neither emphasize nor reject the possibility of an eternal conscious life after death. It *would* emphasize the need for altruism as the most effective policy for self-governance and would assign a great importance to the macro-organism we call the earth, or the biosphere, and its close direct relationship to human welfare and happiness.

"The scientific community needs to be supported by the population at large and given the freedom to explore, hypothesize, experiment, test, and challenge in an objective manner. The political system shall be advised by the scientific community regarding the nature of the physical, chemical, and biological realities of the universe and shall not discard, ignore, or conveniently manipulate these realities when making decisions. Funding and general support of the scientific community shall be independent of the political system or any moneyed interests.

"Societal direction shall be driven not only by the rights of the human citizenry but also the rights of all life systems. Recognizing these are critical for long-term survival of human society and culture. This consideration shall extend to the economic system, which shall take into account currencies that reflect the energy and material flows within our biosphere in addition to the value of human effort as measured by the currency we call money. The economic system shall be driven to be sustainable for the purpose of assuring the privilege of life and liberty not only for ourselves but also our posterity. Long-term impact shall receive preferential consideration over short-term benefits.

"Serious efforts shall be expended to establish a reasonable population management program to ensure that the sustainable economy established can be maintained without reverting to overuse of available resources.

"Rights to life, liberty, and the pursuit of happiness shall be extended to men and women equally and to all races and ethnic groups and persons of all sexual preferences and lifestyles. Rights of other life systems will be delineated and these rights protected as vehemently as human rights. The judicial system shall not be designed to punish but rather protect these rights by identifying, sentencing, confining, and if possible, rehabilitating, through due process of the law, those who abuse the rights of others."

Nadim paused briefly and then continued. "So that is what I envision as the framework of a plausible reformation. It will not happen overnight and likely not with our present leadership. But I already see the movement gaining momentum. I look at my students and students I have met from around the world—intelligent, caring young people, men, women, Jews, Christians, Muslims, Hindus, Buddhists, Taoists, atheists, Shinto, Pantheists, black, white, Asian, European, African, Native Americans, Polynesian, straight, and gay—all able to converse with one another, to respect each other, and most importantly, to see the vision of a sustainable economy and this neo-pantheistic strategy. The change is coming. I just hope, for the sake of Dahlia and all the children and all the earth's species, that it arrives before the catastrophe."

And then there was a prolonged silence. Martha noticed Nadim's voice quivering toward the end of his discourse, and she saw the slight twinkle of tears forming in his eyes. It was very inspiring to see a person so involved and so compassionate. Martha found herself on the verge of crying as well. Finally, Martha let out a deep breath. "You are amazing, Nadim—actually, all of you. Not many families sit around the dinner table and talk like this—I wish they did. It certainly has given me much to think about."

Khalil could tell Martha was quite tired, so he suggested that perhaps it was time to get to bed. "Well, we need to get up fairly early in the morning," he said. "I want to get to the clinic at a reasonable hour so we can get you back to Tel Aviv."

Martha nodded her head, got up, and gave all three of them a hug and then disappeared into the bedroom. She thought the intensity of the conversation would keep her awake, but she found sleep came quickly. She slept soundly until the early morning when Dahlia jumped on her bed. "Martha, Martha, time to wake up!"

CHAPTER 24

Martha awoke refreshed and packed and dressed quickly. When she came into the kitchen, she found Salem preparing breakfast. Soon, Nadim and Khalil arrived. After breakfast, Khalil and Martha packed the car, and after saying good-bye to the others and promising to return as soon as possible, they were off. Both she and Salem were crying, which made Dahlia cry also. Martha had made a real connection with Salem, and she truly hoped their relationship would extend well beyond this one event.

Khalil moved the car slowly into the crowded street and on into Haifa proper. Martha reached over to squeeze Khalil's arm, and he looked at her with a smile. She smiled back without talking.

Martha had made a decision, and she was going to tell Khalil about it later, once they were headed back to Tel Aviv. She had decided to return to Indiana and terminate her marriage with Phil. She was then going to return to Israel, if Khalil agreed, and pursue a relationship with him. If Khalil rejected this idea, then she would make other arrangements for her life. But she knew her marriage was not reparable, nor was it healthy for her or Phil for that matter. Phil had his own demons, and he needed to confront them on his own. Martha being present was not helpful in his facing these challenges. Martha was content with her decision. A new life awaited her—she hoped a life of giving and of love.

Khalil stopped at a rather busy intersection, and that was the last thing Martha recalled before something hit her head with a powerful force—enough to knock her unconscious. And when she awoke, she realized she was kidnapped.

CHAPTER 25

s Martha stood with Fatima overlooking the valley
below from the cave entrance, she suddenly had these
recollections about Khalil and Nadim and his family and
their conversation. Things had changed so much since then. In
fact, when the panic of being kidnapped first hit Martha, she had
not remembered anything about her excursions with Khalil. She
remembered she was in Israel, in Haifa, but fear obliterated most
of these other details. Now, still frightened and fearful but more
collected, Martha's memory returned. She remembered being stopped
at an intersection. That must have been when the men attacked their
car and assaulted and abducted her.

Now, her thoughts turned to Khalil. What happened to him?
Did they kill him? Was he kidnapped also but taken to a separate
place? And then a sickening thought came over her—a thought
that made her knees buckle to the extent that Fatima again had to
catch her. Was Khalil behind the kidnapping? Was he paid to make
American victims like her vulnerable? Is this how he raised money
for his charity? Or perhaps he was part of an extremist group and the

funds went to support their efforts? Was she, at her age, so gullible that she could not detect such things? These thoughts haunted her, and she hoped that they were not true. She began to shake again and to weep softly. Fatima knew she was upset but could only offer gestures of consolation.

When she gained her stability, Fatima led her down a small path. At the base, once they reached the valley floor, she saw a long table, like an oversized picnic bench. Sitting at the table were about twenty women, all dressed as her and Fatima—in rough work clothes with hair drawn back and covered. They were eating breakfast.

Fatima sat down and gestured for Martha to sit next to her, which she did. The women around the table smiled politely but continued eating. Fatima passed a bowl of sliced fruit to Martha. She took several slices of melon and a couple of figs as well and some grapes. She was amazed at how good they tasted. And then there were nuts, bread, and an egg dish and smoked fish and orange juice, as well as goat's milk and coffee—all delicious. *This is not the kind of food I would expect from kidnappers.*

Soon, however, Martha found out why she had been so well fed. As she followed Fatima and the others out into the field, she realized they were here to serve as farmhands. Fatima gave her a large brimmed hat and some type of lotion to protect her skin from the sun. Martha looked around her and noticed a few other men and women working—some picking oranges, some behind oxen tilling the soil, some manipulated the water distribution gates. She also noticed that there were no internal combustion engines anywhere—no tractors or excavators or even trucks. Everything was done by animal or human labor (recognizing, of course, that as Nadim had said, humans are indeed animals as well). Then Martha thought she saw the man who had spoken English to her working in the mango orchard. But it was just a distant glance and she could not be sure.

Fatima apparently had been assigned to train Martha. They started with planting seedlings along a prepared row. It involved straddling the row, bending, making a small hole, placing the seedling, and packing the soil around it. Not difficult, it would seem, but the speed at which Fatima and the others did this amazed Martha. To make it worse, the water bucket and access to a latrine was at the end of each row, so it was required to finish a row before getting a drink or relieving one's self.

Martha was, by American standards, in good physical shape. She did several miles on her stationary bike every day and worked out with light weights in the gym, as well as attended a yoga class twice a week. But exercising in an air-conditioned gym is a great deal different than working all day in an open field as a farm laborer. After about an hour, Martha was improving her planting rate—but still well below that of Fatima. When Fatima finished a row, she stopped and waited for Martha to finish and then gave her a few pointers before they started another row. For three hours, the seedlings kept coming and they kept planting. When they finally finished, Martha realized she had some blisters developing on her hands and feet, and the muscles in her back were beginning to spasm.

During the lunch break, all she wanted to do was lay down. But instead, the women gathered in a circle, held hands and, without any words, meditated for ten minutes—no one moving or making a sound.

After the meditation, the group spent some time relaxing, talking to one another, and laughing quietly. Of course, Martha could not understand a word of what they were saying. She did not even know what language they were speaking. It could have been Arabic of some sort—it did not sound like Hebrew—but then she was hardly an expert. So she listened and smiled politely for fifteen minutes. And then everyone headed back to the fields. This time they were sent to a large cultivated area to pick eggplants—thousands of eggplants. You would think picking eggplants would be easy, but again, there was a knack and a certain rate that was expected. And you have to be certain the eggplant is ready for picking. Martha had to use a small curved knife to disengage the eggplant. It apparently was important to make a clean cut and, of course, avoid cutting the fruit.

Martha wondered how much eggplant was needed to feed this small group. Maybe they were selling it to other villages or to a larger market. Maybe she and the others were captured and put to work as slave labor, thereby increasing the profits. But why would they pick a middle-aged American woman? Certainly younger people would be more efficient. She wondered how much she was worth in this market. Maybe Khalil sold her for a couple hundred bucks—or less? This thought was very upsetting, and she again began to cry. In truth, she had spent most of the day crying. Finally, she just collapsed and sat down. Quickly, Fatima lifted her up.

"Must keep working!" Fatima said. "Must keep working!"

Martha recognized that perhaps she or Fatima or even the whole group of women might be physically punished if she did not continue, so she gestured to Fatima that she was OK and continued with picking eggplants.

After picking eggplants for two hours, they took a twenty-minute break and then finished the day picking tomatoes—something that actually was just as challenging as eggplant harvesting. Finally, Fatima came to her and simply said "Finished," and they walked toward the ridge where the cave entrance was located.

But instead of going directly into the cave, they walked a few hundred yards along a small creek. The water was very clear, and it was evident the source was some type of spring. Back home in Florida, Martha would call this a spring run. As they walked, she recognized a few of the birds—a large heron, a rail-type bird that looked something like what she called a gallinule, and a kingfisher. Finally, they came to the spring boil, which was about three hundred feet across and very deep in the middle. She noticed a bench along the bank stacked with clean clothes, along with some lychees and oranges. All of the women shed their clothes and stacked the dirty laundry in a large pile. Then they all jumped into the spring. Martha followed suit and was soon immersed in the cool water. It reminded her of skinny-dipping in Florida—something her girlfriends and she used to do after spending a few hours drinking contraband whiskey when she was in college.

After about thirty minutes in the water, Martha was shivering, but her muscle aches had subsided somewhat. She stepped out and dried herself off. Fatima came over and gave her a vial of oil and made gestures about working it into her hair. Martha did this and found that, whatever the substance was, it made her hair feel clean and silky. Fatima showed her a large tub of water with which to rinse her hair, which she did. She then put on her clean clothes. While her body was somewhat sore and her hands and feet blistered, she felt surprisingly good.

Just as they were all ready to leave, Fatima rubbed a salve over Martha's cuts and blisters and wrapped them in soft gauze. They then walked back up to the cave entrance. But instead of going to the room where Martha had first been taken, Fatima led her into a large hall that was open at the top, which allowed the sunlight to illuminate the hall. A huge table was set in the middle of the hall. It was obvious they were going to have a communal supper.

Martha thought how similar this community was to a kibbutz or perhaps even closer to an Amish gathering. There were no weapons, and there was no evidence of any modern technology. The people seemed to be happy—although Martha was suspicious about Fatima's earlier concern when Martha stopped working.

What upset Martha the most was that she had no idea where she was or why she had been taken. She was very grateful for Fatima. But while the other women were very polite, she knew nothing about them. And of course, she could not communicate. The only person who apparently could talk to her was the leader, if indeed he was the leader. If he was the leader, why would he be out working with everyone else? Was this community that egalitarian?

There was one thing Martha could say about this place—the food was extraordinary. The supper included chicken baked in some delicious spices with a variety of vegetables and wild rice and an eggplant dish, along with a Mediterranean-type salad. The most impressive, however, was the fruit—especially the lychee and the mangoes, which were like sweet golden velvet. And there was no limit to how much you could eat.

She noticed that over one hundred people shared supper in this hall tonight. This was a great deal more people than just the few she had seen today—which perhaps had been no more than thirty. She wondered if this was just one subcommunity because the land under cultivation appeared quite extensive.

Martha's imagination had finally determined that this operation was indeed Hezbollah or, at least, Hezbollah-supported. The excess crops were likely used to support their security and military effort and perhaps for charity. The workers did not seem to be Muslim, for she saw no Mosque, nor were there calls to prayer. Actually, outside of the meditation circle, she saw no indication of any religion—no crosses, no Star of David, no crescent. The only thing she did remember was the respect the leader had shown the Prophet Muhammad during their conversation. *He was probably Muslim*, she thought, *and perhaps a few of the others at the top of the social hierarchy. I guess it would make some sense that they would kidnap only non-believers. These they might justify as deserving of slavery.*

But as overseers to a slave workforce, they were comparatively kind. Martha wondered if Fatima and the other women were married—did they have children? She had seen no children—but then she had been here only one full day, and her mind and her body were still in a state of shock and disbelief, and her needing to know what was happening to her was continually tormenting her.

After supper, Fatima led Martha back to the room she had been taken originally. She was shown a small cot with linens and a pillow. She also noted a bowl of water and the same powder she had used to clean her teeth. She washed her face then cleaned her teeth best she could and lay down to sleep. She slept soundly.

As the morning before, Fatima woke her just before daybreak. They followed the same routine, and within thirty minutes, they were again at the breakfast table. Martha assumed that they would be working in the fields again. But instead, they walked about half a mile to the south to the goat pen.

"Milk goats," Fatima said in English and then repeated it in her language—whatever that was. Obviously, Fatima wanted Martha to learn her language, which gave hint to Martha that she might be here a while.

Of course, Martha had never milked a goat in her life. The next couple of hours, therefore, were quite humorous, particularly for Fatima, who tried to teach Martha how to first capture the lactating goats and then move them into an isolation pen. Fatima was very skilled at cornering the goats and slipping a crude halter over their head. Martha soon discovered that this was not that easy.

Finally, they had about ten goats in the pen, each with a halter. Of the ten goats, Martha had captured one, and that was done with great difficulty. Fatima then took one of the goats—one of the more cooperative individuals—and put her on a platform and placed her head through a slotted board with a bucket of grain conveniently placed so she could eat while they milked her.

Like the capturing, Fatima made the milking look easy. But Martha had trouble holding the teat correctly and squeezing it properly, allowing it to discharge, then refill. For Fatima, it was second nature, and she did two teats at a time, alternating their discharge and refill in a rhythm. With Martha's inexperience, it took them quite a long time to finish, but Fatima remained patient. When they went after the second batch of goats, Martha was starting to get the hang of it. She would hear Fatima's muzzled giggle whenever she would fall or slip or get outsmarted by a goat, and Martha, for a brief moment, felt that she was actually having fun.

In just one night, Martha's blisters had begun to heal, and to her surprise, they did not hurt while she was milking the goats. Also, she felt her muscles adapting to the demands of the work with new muscles being tested and responding. She was still sore, but it was not intolerable.

When they were through with the goats, they poured most of the milk in a large receptacle. Martha assumed it would be used to make cheese. Fatima took some of the milk, however, and filled two smaller containers, and then they walked to the spring run and placed them in the cool water. Martha assumed these would be used for midday lunch and perhaps for breakfast in the morning.

After their lunch break, they went to the chicken pens and fed the hens and collected any eggs that had not been gathered in the morning. Then they began cleaning the coops and gathering the feathers and manure, which were stacked up into a pile. Once they had a large pile, they shoveled it into a couple of handcarts, which they rolled about a quarter of a mile to the composting area. Here, they emptied the manure and blended it with straw and laid the mix out on a windrow. Martha could feel the heat and steam coming off of the adjoining compost piles. A man was there attending to the rows, mixing them periodically, adding water and straw and stockpiling finished compost for final cure. The final product was apparently moved back into the field to provide nutrients for the crops.

As with the day before, Martha and Fatima ended the day with a bath at the spring boil. And again, this was followed up by a communal supper in the large hall with the open top. While she was eating, the leader, as she had come to call him, came over to talk with her.

"Fatima tells me you are learning quickly although you are still rather slow," he said. Martha thought she could detect a slight smile. She was still a long way from liking this man.

"I thought I worked pretty damned fast for a women who just two days earlier was kidnapped and drugged," she replied without looking directly at him. "When are you going to tell me what you intend to do with me?"

Then she started to cry again. *The man still smells horrible, like three-day-old garlic and an old T-shirt. Fatima does not smell like that. What was with the men in this place? They were disgusting,* she thought.

He leaned over so she had to look directly into his eyes. "I told you we do not answer questions, Mrs. Browning," he whispered. "Just keep working, and try to learn the language."

Martha was about ready to ask what the language was, but she realized that would be a question and he would not answer. "I think I have decided to not work until you tell me what you intend to do with me," she said in a rather loud voice bordering on a scream. She thought, *Well, there is a statement that is not a question.*

"And just how long do you think you can go without food? Remember, Mrs. Browning, it is your choice whether you live or die. Those who wish to enjoy the fruits of our collective efforts must work. Just stay with Fatima and trust her. I will check back with you in a couple of days," he commented, and then with a smile, he turned and left.

Martha could not really say that the man was mean, but he was stern in an unemotional sort of way. Cold perhaps best described his mannerisms. She had the feeling he saw her as an investment—nothing more, nothing less. Kind of the same attitude you might expect from a slaveholder toward a slave he just purchased.

Martha really wanted to have a different opinion of this guy, but that was difficult because she had no solid information upon which to substantiate such a shift in her feelings. She was confused because Fatima and the other women were so nice, and yet this guy was so aloof. Was he evil, or was he good? Well, he was a kidnapper—so in her mind the good option was eliminated.

CHAPTER 26

What was most bizarre to Martha was that even after only two days, she was actually starting to enjoy herself. She thought about her past and came to realize that, in spite of her some fifty-plus years of living and all the people she had dealt with, the only people she really missed were her son, Khalil, Salem, Nadim, and Dahlia. And it made her sad that she may never see them again. But if she was indeed going to be in this place for a long time, she thought she might as well adapt. And she was adapting, and she was finding that the work and even the nonverbal relationships were both invigorating and restorative. She did miss thoughtful conversations like the one she had enjoyed with Nadim, Khalil, and Salem, but she imagined those would come once she became more comfortable with the language.

And of course, there was Fatima, her link to sanity. Martha's admiration for Fatima was growing. She was kind, agile, and very tolerant of Martha's ineptitude. She did not know what would happen if for some reason she lost access to Fatima.

For the next few days, the routine continued. Then one morning, Fatima arrived late. She was dressed in somewhat nicer clothes and brought similar type clothes for Martha. When she was finished dressing, Martha followed Fatima to the entrance of the cavern. They walked down to the valley floor and walked another mile to the north along a small path. Finally, they came upon another spring but much larger than the spring they bathed in. About three hundred people were spread out around the spring. There were indeed children and families. And the women wore no coverings for their hair. Some of the men were bearded while some were clean-shaven, and several were bare-chested. People, especially the children, were going in and out of the water. Apparently, it was to be a day free from work—a weekend of sorts.

Fatima led Martha to a small bench where a tall lean man of about thirty was sitting. As they approached, he stood up and smiled at Martha.

"Hassan, my husband," Fatima said with a smile, and then she repeated the introduction in her language.

Martha nodded her head and extended her hand. She hoped this was the proper greeting. "Very nice to meet you, Hassan," Martha said. Hassan took her hand and then gave Martha a big hug, which surprised her. These people have Middle Eastern names and look Middle Eastern, but they do not behave always in a Middle Eastern manner. But then Martha thought she should not be prone to such stereotypes. Anyway, Hassan's hug was sincere and appreciated.

Fatima then introduced Martha to their two children, Nadia, a gangly girl of about eight, and a four-year-old boy named Ibrahim. They quickly offered their politeness and then scurried off to play with the other children.

For most of the day, Martha ate and lay on a blanket, taking in the sun and the mild breeze. She also tried to talk some with Hassan and Fatima in their language, but that did not work out too well although she was making progress. Many times they laughed at her faulty pronunciation. The sounds were difficult for her to make, but she was determined to keep trying.

It turned out to be a delightful day, ending with a simple meal just before sunset. As they were leaving, Fatima came to Martha and very slowly, in Fatima's language, said what Martha thought was "Bad job tomorrow. See you then." She repeated it slowly to Fatima, who acknowledge with a nod.

"OK," Martha said. "See you in the morning."

And then they walked back to the cavern entrance. Martha, as before, found sleep quite easily.

CHAPTER 27

F atima awakened Martha as usual in the morning. After
breakfast, however, their group moved back up the path to
the cavern entrance, taking a number of handcarts and tools
with them. They first went into the large hallway where they typically
ate supper. A large amount of straw had been dropped through the
top opening and was piled on the floor of the room. Each cart was
attended by two women.

Fatima and Martha loaded up their handcart with straw and
rolled the cart down one of the passageways and eventually into one
of the trench latrines. Martha now was beginning to understand
what "bad job" meant.

After donning a moist cloth mask over their mouth and nose,
they began filling the trench with straw and used long-handled hoes
to mix the straw into the waste. The straw had been chopped into
fibers about four to six inches, so it blended and compacted well.
After the straw was mixed thoroughly, they returned to the hallway
to get more straw. And so they kept adding and mixing straw until the
moisture was well absorbed. And while the moisture was absorbed,

the smell was not. Martha felt herself on several occasions getting nauseated. But the worst was yet to come.

After about two hours, they had the waste-straw mixture well homogenized down the entire length. Now, Fatima indicated they had to remove it. They did this with a special two-person long-handled scraper, which allowed them to move a portion of the mixture up a sloped end into the handcart that had been set in a bunker to facilitate capture of the material. When the handcart was full, they hauled it back to the cave entrance, down the road to the valley, and about a quarter of a mile northwest to another composting facility—not the same facility that they took the chicken manure to last week.

Two men were managing this facility, and Martha was surprised that it did not smell as bad as she expected. The men were constantly mixing the compost rows and adding straw and other fiber, as well as water, as they felt necessary. The rows emitted large amounts of steam and were obviously very hot. She suspected they operated the rows in this manner so all the pathogenic organisms were destroyed. She suspected that the final product would be used as fertilizer. By American standards, this seemed disgusting, but the use of such night soils throughout the world was quite common. Martha remembered actually reading about this at sometime in her past. This was, however, the first time she had seen it actually being processed. Obviously, if the community did not purchase outside fertilizers, they have to make a real effort to recycle nutrients, particularly phosphorus, potassium, and a few of the trace metals. Nitrogen they could largely recover by rotating crops with legumes such as soybeans.

After about six hours of working with only brief breaks, Martha and Fatima had totally removed the waste material from the trench and had cleaned all the handcarts and tools. This meant they had some extra time at the spring. They knew they probably smelled pretty bad, so it was going to feel extra nice to get clean. Martha soaked for an extra half hour in the water even though she was almost blue when she finally got out. Then she and Fatima lay down on the soft grass and gazed up at the blueness of the sky and attempted to have a conversation in Fatima's language. Martha was learning, but they still had to repeat things several times for the other to understand, and Fatima often had to use gestures or sign language to convey the meaning of certain words or phrases. Through the conversation, Martha did learn that latrine cleaning was only a once-a-month requirement. For that she was thankful.

CHAPTER 28

And so the days passed, and the routine changed little, except that it seemed they had a different task every day. The leader had talked to her several times, and Martha found his presence more tolerable with each visit although she still was not certain if he could be trusted. Martha had not done a real good job of keeping up with the passing time, but she figured that she had been there perhaps six months. It was becoming clear that she may be spending her remaining life here—there was no indication that a ransom had been paid or even sought. She had hoped Khalil would have made inquiries about her and perhaps would eventually determine her location. But she did not know if he was even alive or perhaps also a kidnap victim. And of course, even though she did not wish to think of it, it was possible he was part of the kidnapping plot.

Martha was somewhat depressed about the turn of events, but she was becoming used to the communal farm life, and she now had a pretty good grasp of the language—although she still did not know what language it was. She also had found out that the forbidding of asking questions extended to everyone. When she would ask Fatima about the place or the leader or how long she had been there, all she got was an apology that she could not answer any questions. Of course, they could have long conversations about kids and husbands and the weather and the identification of certain birds or their favorite flowers, and this did help. But there remained a frustration regarding her fate and the purpose of her being taken.

And so Martha embraced acceptance of her fate. She was healthy; she was among people who cared for her, and she spent most of her time in the glorious outdoors. She had the best food she could imagine, and she kept herself clean and comfortable. It was not the worst life.

CHAPTER 29

A nd then one morning, the leader came to Martha just as they were leaving from breakfast.

"Come with me, Martha," he said in English. He had finally quit calling her Mrs. Browning, at least.

Martha walked with the leader for about forty-five minutes to the south until the path opened up into a wider road. The leader stopped and pointed to a person standing about two hundred yards away. She could tell it was a man, but it was too far for her to recognize who it was.

"You can go if you wish. He is waiting for you," the leader said, gesturing toward the man.

Martha was shocked. Six months of not knowing and now she was offered her freedom! Was that Khalil waiting for her? She hoped so. Perhaps it was Phil? She began walking and then started to run.

At about fifty yards, she saw that it was indeed Phil. She ran into his embrace and exclaimed, "You finally found me, thank God."

"Better to thank the Israeli police," Phil said coldly. He held her, but not with any compassion. She could tell he was upset, which she thought was reasonable to an extent. But he certainly showed little excitement in finally finding her.

"We had no idea what happened to you. Look at you! You look so brown and skinny. And you do not smell real good, to be honest. And what were you doing in the car with that Palestinian? Were you screwing him? Tell me what is going on with you. Our daughter is worse than ever." (He always referred to his daughter as their daughter.) Everyone at the church is sick with concern. And I come to Israel to find you are having an affair with an Arab—a Palestinian Arab. Was he a terrorist?" Phil bombarded her with question after question, which made her very anxious. For the first time in six months, she could feel stress tightening up her stomach.

"Phil, I know you are upset, but aren't you happy to see me? Aren't you happy I am alive and healthy?" Martha responded. "I can explain my excursion with Khalil and his family. I can assure you, I was not having an affair."

But Phil did not let up. It was one charge after another, often followed by degrading vulgarities. Finally, Martha began crying.

"Please, Phil, this has been quite an ordeal for me. I did not know where I was or what was going to happen to me. Now, I have an opportunity to go back home. Don't be so hateful," Martha sobbed.

"Well, you can come home, but things are going to change. No more trips to Israel, and I am going to expect you to help our daughter more. I cannot figure out what is wrong with her," Phil said.

"You—you are what is wrong with her! You enable her. I think you do it on purpose so you can keep her under control!" Martha exclaimed.

With this accusation, Phil briskly struck Martha with the back of his hand. She fell to the ground and looked up at him in shock. He had never hit her before. He had threatened, but this was the first time he actually hit her. But she had never challenged him like this before either. She knew he had this mean streak in him—and she had learned how to avoid it.

Martha stayed in a kneeling position and thought seriously about telling Phil she did not want to go home with him. But that would be a hard decision. After months of not knowing anything, she now had an opportunity to return to something she did know—even if it was not perfect, it was home.

Just as she started to get up, she felt something behind her. She stood up and looked over her shoulder. What she saw sent an electric shock through her body. It was the dog from her childhood—the mangy, emaciated dog of her dreams. How could that be?

And Martha looked at the dog, and she felt love. Phil had picked up a stick to chase off the dog.

"Get out of here, you ugly mutt. Go away and die somewhere!" he screamed.

But Martha stopped him and then knelt next to the dog, and in spite of his smell and his open sores and his trembling, she put her arms around him and pulled him to her.

"Don't worry, we will take care of you. You do not need to be scared," she said softly. Then she turned to confront Phil. But he was gone.

CHAPTER 30

Martha remained with the dog. She assumed Phil had left in disgust, but for some reason, it did not bother her. She was more concerned about the dog. Phil had his own demons to tend too, and she had, some time ago, realized he needed to do this without her.

"I see you have decided to live, Martha." It was the voice of the leader who was now standing next to her. "Shall we walk back?"

"Yes," Martha whispered.

She noticed the sun reflecting off the forming clouds, which generated an aura of extraordinary light. And all frustrations left her, and all questions were answered, and she felt content and happy—truly happy.

She looked at the leader then said, "I understand now."

"No questions?" the leader asked.

"They are all answered. No need for any questions," she answered.

"Then you know Khalil had nothing to do with your being brought to this place?" he said.

"Yes. I know that," she replied. She also knew why the leader happened to know Khalil.

On the way back, she felt love and happiness like she had never experienced, and she realized that she was truly loving and truly loved. She looked forward to bringing her new dog back to health.

CHAPTER 31

Dan Stein had moved to Israel in the nineties from New York after having been with the NYPD for fifteen years. It was always his wife's dream to live in Israel, and after their son moved from home, Dan felt he owed it to her to move. Besides, he had always liked the idea as well. New York was his home, his birthplace, but he also felt an allegiance to Israel.

And he enjoyed it immensely. They both already spoke Hebrew, so the language was not a problem. But after a year, he began to miss police work, so he managed to get a job in Haifa with the Israeli police. He had actually worked his way up to inspector. The challenges in Israel were somewhat different than New York, and the hierarchy and culture were also different. But he got used to it and was now looking to work perhaps two more years before retiring.

Investigating events that involved American citizens were not Dan's favorite part of the job. If it was serious enough, it usually meant working with the American consulate, and it was typical that he would eventually have to deal with concerned and often irate

E. Allen Stewart III

relatives who had been notified and who often had to disrupt their schedules to come to Israel.

Such was the case Dan was called to investigate on Thursday morning. When he arrived, several people were already managing the site. It involved an American woman and an Arab doctor—a strange combination, Dan thought. The representative of the American consulate had been called and was already there when Dan arrived. They had recovered the woman's passport and had notified her husband, who lived in Indiana. He apparently was planning on coming to Israel.

The doctor was a Khalil Suleiman, who was sitting with a couple of people, who Dan guessed to be relatives, on the side of the intersection. He appeared to be relatively unharmed. Dan had heard of Dr. Suleiman—if he recalled, he was involved with some sort of a radical group. Dan would have to investigate this closely as security would want to know the complete story of the rendezvous between this American woman and Dr. Suleiman.

The woman's name was Martha Browning, from Indiana of all places. What was she doing in Haifa with an Arab radical? Dan asked if they might get him a copy of her passport. He apparently had some work to do.

It was actually a very tragic accident. The red Renault had been sitting at the intersection when the delivery truck swerved out of its lane, doing about 35 mph (Dan still had the habit of converting kmh to mph.) It hit the passenger's side without braking. Dr. Suleiman survived, but the woman was killed instantly.